Praise for *Blood Rite* by Trista Ann Michaels

"*Blood Rite* is a wonderful paranormal romance that I could not put down! This is a fast moving story that grabs you by throat and does not let go until you have read the very last page."

– Regina, *Coffee Time Romance*

"Trista Ann Michaels effortlessly weaves an intense and emotionally charged tale that is sure to please paranormal and erotica fans alike."

– Heather, *Fallen Angel Reviews*

"This author is a master who always delivers a fresh, delightful, and emotional story that is well crafted and brimming with intense and deliciously daring characters along with a plot that has devilish twists and turns… Trista Ann Michaels is an author who continues to delight her fans by delivering a scorching and memorable story no matter what genre she writing in."

– Shannon, *The Romance Studio*

"Ms. Michaels once again delivers a sexy hit!"

– T. S. Peters, *Just Erotic Romance Reviews*

LooseId®

ISBN 13: 978-1-60737-403-9
BLOOD RITE
Copyright © December 2009 by Trista Ann Michaels
Originally released in e-book format in March 2009

Cover Art by Christine M. Griffin
Cover Layout and Design by April Martinez

All rights reserved. Except for use of brief quotations in any review or critical article, the reproduction or utilization of this work in whole or in part in any form by any electronic, mechanical or other means, now known or hereafter invented, including xerography, photocopying and recording, or in any information storage or retrieval is forbidden without the prior written permission of Loose Id LLC, PO Box 425960, San Francisco CA 94142-5960. http://www.loose-id.com

DISCLAIMER: Many of the acts described in our BDSM/fetish titles can be dangerous. Please do not try any new sexual practice, whether it be fire, rope, or whip play, without the guidance of an experienced practitioner. Neither Loose Id nor its authors will be responsible for any loss, harm, injury or death resulting from use of the information contained in any of its titles.

This book is an original publication of Loose Id. Each individual story herein was previously published in e-book format only by Loose Id and is a work of fiction. Any similarity to actual persons, events or existing locations is entirely coincidental.

Printed in the U.S.A. by
Lightning Source, Inc.
1246 Heil Quaker Blvd
La Vergne TN 37086
www.lightningsource.com

BLOOD RITE

Prologue

Vlad closed the lid of the tomb, sealing the skeleton off from the cold air of the room. No one should find him here. At least until the time was right.

"It won't be long now, Sebastian."

In two years, Sebastian's daughter would be twenty-five, and her vampire genes would begin to emerge. On the day of her ascension, they would bring her here where her blood would rejuvenate their leader—the future ruler of the new dark world. A world where vampires would reign as kings and mortals would exist only as food.

Chapter One

Standing just inside the door of the castle, Julian watched with growing anger as Sebastian attacked his son, Marcus. His fingers clenched around the handle of the crossbow as indecision waged a battle within him. Should he intervene? His son would be furious, but Julian could never live with himself if anything happened to him. An eternity was a long time to have to deal with regret. He already had one regret—not fighting harder for Marcus's mother—and he didn't need another one.

Raising the crossbow, he took aim at Sebastian's back.

"Marcus, look out," a woman screamed.

His finger pulled the trigger, but at the last second, just before the arrow would have pierced his heart, Sebastian shifted. The arrow went through Sebastian's chest, only grazing his heart and barely missing his son in the process. Julian's heart almost stopped.

The vampire Sebastian fell to the floor, his whole body trembling in shock and pain.

"Julian," he gasped.

Raising his gaze, he caught his son staring at him, his eyes narrowed, his nostrils flared in anger. God, he looked so much like him, but in all other things, he was definitely his mother.

"Did you mean to hit me or him?"

Julian stiffened. "Don't be ridiculous."

Yes, he and his son had their differences, but surely he knew he would never try to kill him.

The room shifted, changed as darkness closed in around him. Coldness seeped into his bones, piercing them with the sharp blades of icy premonition. He knew this feeling. Witchcraft. Someone was trying to speak to him...warn him.

"Julian," a soft voice whispered through his mind, and he closed his eyes as pain wrapped around his heart.

Kayla, his son's mother, the love of his life.

No, this couldn't be happening. She'd been dead for over four hundred years.

"It's time, Julian. Time to let go of your pain."

He shook his head. He didn't want to. He couldn't.

"There's a war coming, Julian. A terrible war. She needs you."

"Who needs me?" he demanded.

"Trust in your heart. Trust in her. Help her."

"Who?" he yelled.

Her presence faded and he struggled to hold on to it, struggled to keep her with him for just a little while longer. He missed her so much.

"Kayla," he whispered.

"You belong with her, Julian." Her voice came across stronger this time, more forceful.

He shook his head, intending to argue, but her presence was gone. A feeling of utter emptiness engulfed him, and he closed his eyes against the pain. Sounds invaded his mind, voices he couldn't place, words he couldn't decipher. A sense of danger crept through his chest, tightening his muscles. The smell of death and blood filled his senses and he growled, his fangs dropping into place as hunger and the need to feed raced through him.

Over a thousand years of instinct took over as he prepared for battle, for the vampires he could feel closing in around him. A woman screamed in the distance, calling him. He cocked his head to better listen, to try and pinpoint where it came from.

"She needs you, Julian."

Julian awoke with a start and stared around the dusk-filled room, his body tense and ready for battle. *What the hell was that?* Once satisfied no one occupied the room with him, he relaxed and swung his legs off the bed. With a tired sigh, he stood and strolled naked to the window. Opening the thick velvet curtains, he watched as the last rays of sunlight dipped behind the mountains of his Romanian home.

A coldness permeated the castle as night fell, chilling his flesh. Below him, his gaze caught that of his friend, Andre. In wolf form, his white fur stood out against the darkening horizon, his gold-green eyes sparkling with intelligence.

"*Are you up for some hunting, Andre?*" he asked in his mind.

The wolf nodded, then turned to howl toward the moon. Although Andre never fed off their victims like Julian did, he enjoyed the hunt. The two of them would find a willing female, engage in a night of ménage sex where Julian would feed just enough to satisfy his hunger, leaving the woman dazed and remembering nothing of the night before except the sex.

It was a strategy that had worked well over the centuries, keeping suspicion at bay. Turning from the window, he tried to push the remnants of the dream from his mind. Kayla had been a powerful witch and could do many things, but he doubted contact from the dead was one of them.

* * *

Addison Gray strolled through the streets of the French Quarter, a feeling of danger wrapping around her like a cloak. The sensation of dread had begun with the dreams, dreams of a man with long black hair and eyes so deep blue they left her breathless, and a woman's voice telling her "he needs you." But around this man also lurked danger so strong it made her stomach tighten in fear.

The dreams were just one of many things that had begun to change in her life. Her mother was a witch, her father… Well, she had no idea *who* her father was, but she knew *what* he was. A vampire.

She knew the signs of change. She'd seen it before in other half-breed children. There weren't many, and the change affected them all in different ways. Some became full vampires, sensitive to light and with a hunger for blood.

Some merely carried the physical traits—the ethereal beauty and fangs. Day walkers was what they were called. She had no idea yet what her fate would be; it had only just begun and she needed answers, help. And she knew just who to turn to.

Marcus Delacroix, half-breed son of witch Kayla Delacroix and vampire Julian Petri. Despite his status as a day walker, he was a close ally of the witch's council, both very highly respected as a wizard and highly feared as a vampire. He and his wife, Tonya, would know what to do for her.

After two weeks of looking, she'd finally tracked him down to New Orleans. He had a house in the Garden District, just a few blocks from the French Quarter. She could hop the trolley and be there in less than an hour.

A sense of being watched ran through her, and the hairs on the back of her neck stood on end. She stopped and glanced nervously at the crowd. This feeling had plagued her for weeks now—as though someone waited in the shadows, watching, calculating. She scanned the faces, seeing nothing in them that would cause her harm or fear. She shook off the sensation and picked up her pace toward the trolley stop.

Jumping onto the trolley, she took a seat toward the front and tried to think about what she would say to him.

I think I'm turning. I need your help? How do I tell if I will be full or half?

She hadn't yet developed a sensitivity to light or a hunger for blood, but her fangs had descended twice now. Once when she was angry and once when she was afraid. Even now, she felt the urge rushing through her to snarl and bare her fangs. Taking a deep breath, she ran her tongue over the sharp edges of her canines. Blood filled her mouth from the shallow cut across her tongue. The warm, metallic taste made her sigh, and she tensed against the feeling of euphoria that coursed through her veins.

That had never happened. Was that one of the signs? Would she crave blood? Her lips tightened as her jaw set in anger. She didn't want to change. She didn't want to become a hunter, a feeder. She didn't want to be ruled by the hunger, controlled by it. She had to find a way to fight this.

* * *

Julian licked his tongue across the bite mark of the young woman dangling between him and Andre. Both their cocks were buried deep inside her, his in her ass, Andre's in her pussy. The warmth in her flesh faded as he sipped one last time from her neck, savoring the metallic taste as it surged through his own veins, quieting his hunger.

She shivered and he stopped before he went too far. She was already cold; it wouldn't take much to kill her completely.

"It's almost dawn," Andre murmured. "You need to get back to the castle. I'll take care of her."

Nodding, he pulled his cock from her warm body and quickly grabbed his clothes. He'd clean up at home, then sleep. When he awoke tomorrow, his hunger would be gone, at least for a while. He could then focus more on this dream and the threat of war.

What war could it be? Sebastian had been killed two years ago, the threat to the witch's council demolished with his death. Was it possible his followers had taken up where he left off?

The ramifications of such a war were staggering. Humans would no longer be ignorant of their existence. Wizards, vampires, werewolves would be brought from fantasy to reality. It was something Julian refused to accept, which unfortunately had become a minority opinion among the undead. Over the last few years, vampires had become bolder, no longer content to leave their victims breathing and cloudy of the night's events. They wanted to taste the last drop, the sweetness that filled them as their victim's heart jerked with its last beat.

Even Julian could admit to the euphoria that followed, but he'd learned to fight it, to resist. Others had not.

Stepping into the back door of his castle, he made his way quickly through the kitchen and dining area, then toward the foyer and the stairs that would lead him to his darkened bedchamber. As he entered the foyer, the hairs on the back of his neck stood on end. He slowed, his gaze taking in the mahogany-paneled room and shining Italian tiled floors. Standing at the foot of his stairs was the cause of his sudden tenseness.

Her black cape covered her from neck to toe. Blonde hair cascaded around her shoulders in soft waves as she turned to stare at him, her eyes full of worry. It must be important if she would use magic to enter his home. Everyone on the council knew he forbade it. But for Rebecca, he would let it go.

"Madam Councilwoman," he acknowledged, placing his hand on the banister and leaning on it slightly. As dawn approached, some of his strength began to vanish.

She made a face, crinkling her nose. "Rebecca, please."

"All right. Rebecca. What are you doing here?"

"I know it's late for you. But I need to ask you about Sebastian."

Now it was Julian's turn to curl his lip.

"I know that the two of you were…"

"Lovers?" he finished for her, his lips twitching in amusement.

She sighed. "I'm sorry, okay. I just can't picture a man as masculine as you having sex with another man."

Julian chuckled. "I have sex with women too, more so than men." He shrugged. "I get bored sometimes. Now what did you want to know?"

"Did he ever mention having a child to you?"

He stood straighter. "A child?"

"Yes. There's talk of a blood rite. Please, if you know anything…"

Julian sat on one of the stairs and rested his elbows on his knees. Shaking his head, he replied, "Sebastian never mentioned a child."

Rebecca sat down next to him with a sigh.

"What makes you think it's Sebastian?" he asked.

"It's a rumor. Other vampires have heard talk on the streets."

Julian nodded, his own thoughts returning to his dream. Did the warning have something to do with this blood rite?

"Tell me something," he demanded.

"What?"

"Can a witch make contact from the dead?"

She blinked in surprise, then her eyes narrowed. "Did Sebastian contact you, Julian?"

"No. Kayla did."

"Kayla? But she's been dead over four hundred years."

"Is it possible?"

"Yes, through black magic. What did she say to you?"

He sighed and brushed his hair back off his shoulder. "She warned me of a war."

"Then perhaps the talk is correct." Her eyes widened. "We need to find that child. But we don't know if it's a boy or a girl."

Julian pursed his lips, thinking back to the dream and all that was said. "I bet it's a girl."

Rebecca spun to stare at him. "Why?"

He smiled slightly, dreading what he knew was about to be dropped on his doorstep. "Because Kayla said, '*she* needs you.'"

Shaking her head, Rebecca's pretty face scrunched into a frown. "She could have meant me…needing your help."

"No," Julian said, his shoulders drooping slightly. "She meant the child."

"I can perform a spell and find her."

He turned to look at Rebecca. She watched him expectantly, almost warily. She was such a beautiful woman and had grown as a witch so much in the last couple of years. With a nod, he relented and she smiled in thanks.

"Is there anything of Sebastian's still here?" she asked. "I'll need it."

He inclined his head toward the upper landing. "Upstairs, third door on the right. When you're done, I'll be in my chamber."

She nodded and headed quickly up the stairs.

Chapter Two

Addison stood outside Marcus's house, staring at it from the sidewalk. Huge oak trees shaded the two-story house. White columns stood across the front like sentient guards protecting all who dwelled within. Wicker furniture lined the front porch, giving the home an inviting atmosphere and making it a little easier for her to approach. Taking a deep breath, she made her way up the walkway to the front door.

Knocking, she waited for someone to answer. Through the beveled glass, she could make out a slender figure as it approached the door. It swung open and a smiling, utterly beautiful young woman greeted her. She wore a slinky black dress, showing off her curvy figure to perfection. Her dark blonde hair was pulled back in a loose knot, tiny tendrils of corkscrew curls framing her face and green eyes sparkling happily. Addison would give anything to be that happy.

"Hello. Can I help you?"

Addison blinked, silently reminding herself why she was here. "I'm sorry. Are you Tonya?"

"Yes."

"Then I have the right house? I'm looking for Marcus."

Her smile faded somewhat and was replaced by a look of concern as she studied her. Addison's hands tightened around the strap of her purse.

"Come in," Tonya said as she stepped aside, allowing Addison to step into the oversize entry hall.

Tonya shut the door, then turned to again study her. Addison tried to appear as steady as possible, letting her gaze wander around the antique-filled room. It was absolutely stunning.

"Are all these moldings the originals?" she asked.

Tonya smiled softly and Addison got the impression she could trust her. "Yes, but somehow, I don't think you came here to talk about the moldings. Are you okay?"

She sighed and turned to face Tonya fully. "I don't know. Are you one of them?"

Tonya raised an eyebrow, but otherwise appeared totally unaffected by the questions. "One of who?"

"You're turning, aren't you?"

Addison jumped and turned to stare at the man who'd spoken. He stood halfway down the stairs and watched her with eyes just like the ones from her dreams. Although he had dark hair as well, she knew instinctively he wasn't the man she'd dreamed of. She watched him with a frown as he descended the stairs. His black hair was cropped short, accentuating his rugged face and strong jaw. The white shirt and black pants outlined a wide chest and narrow waist any man would kill for and most any woman would lust after.

"Yes. I'm turning. I'll be twenty-five in about a month, and I'm starting to feel the effects of the change."

He nodded as he reached the bottom step. "They'll worsen the closer you get to ascension. Which one was the vampire? Your mother or father?"

"Father, but I don't know his name. My mother was a witch, but she died two years ago."

"Sounds like you," Tonya said with a slight grin. "Mother is a witch, father a vampire."

"But when I turn will I be like you?" Addison asked.

Marcus shrugged one shoulder and crossed his arms over his chest. "That's hard to say. We won't know until you fully ascend, but truthfully there are very few like me. Most fully turn."

A tear slipped from the corner of her eye to slide down her cheek. She wiped it away quickly, refusing to fall into despair just yet. Tonya rushed forward and grabbed her arm. "What's your name, honey?"

"Addison Gray."

"Do you want some coffee or tea? The three of us can go in the kitchen and talk."

Addison nodded. "That would be great, thank you."

Marcus followed along behind them, silent for the most part while Tonya put on water for tea. Through the window, she could see the sun setting and her apprehension returned. A tightening in her chest always followed the rise of darkness.

"I'm so sorry. You two look as though you were about to go out."

Tonya waved her hand in dismissal. "Don't worry about it. We have centuries yet to go out."

With a grin, Addison took the cup Tonya handed her. The two of them definitely made a stunning couple.

"Who sent you here?" Marcus asked.

"No one sent me. I tracked you down on my own."

"I can't stop it, Addison."

"I know. I just didn't know what to expect." Glancing down at her cup, she pursed her lips briefly. "I'm afraid I don't know any vampires personally."

Marcus chuckled. "You make it sound like it's a flaw."

"Sorry," she said, half grinning. "It's frightening."

"Yes. And I'm afraid to say it will get even more so. You're basically going to die, Addison."

She gasped, staring at him wide-eyed.

"Marcus," Tonya chastised.

He leaned forward, resting his elbows on the table. "She needs to know this, sweet."

Addison swallowed. "I'm really going to die?"

"In a manner of speaking, yes. Your body is going to change. It will no longer need the things it needs now. Air, water, even food. If you turn fully, you'll become sensitive to sunlight. The process, though, is painful."

"What about once I turn? How will I know how to survive? What I need to do?"

"You should have a mentor," Tonya offered. "What about Julian?"

Marcus raised an eyebrow and snorted. "You're kidding, right?"

"Why not?"

"She's a witch, that's why not. Remember, you've met the man."

Tonya rolled her eyes. She'd heard of Julian's aversion to witchcraft and members of the council. Most everyone had.

"It's interesting he hates the council, but he's usually the one they run to when there's a problem," Tonya said, lifting her cup to take a sip of tea.

"Yeah, I've noticed that too," Marcus said with a snicker. "Maybe one day we'll know the reason behind it."

Addison looked at him in surprise. "You don't know?"

"No," he said, shaking his head. "My father and I are not on the best of terms. He doesn't like my wizard side."

"If he hates witches so much, how did he end up with your mother?" she asked in curiosity.

"That's the million-dollar question."

"I have a theory," Tonya offered. "I think he was in love with Marcus's mother. When she couldn't bring herself to let him turn her, he turned his back on everything that reminded him of her. And that included witchcraft."

Marcus smiled, making the lines around his eyes deepen. "Always the romantic, aren't you?"

Shrugging one shoulder, Tonya placed the cup back in its saucer. "It's a good theory. Anyway, we need to get back to Addison."

"I agree." Clasping his hands, he turned his full attention to Addison. "You'll need to find somewhere to go, somewhere that has a basement or darkened interior room just in case you fully turn. You'll know instinctively. If you're full, you'll have an instinct to avoid the sun. I've never dealt with the hunger, so I'm afraid I can't help you there, but I do know you can feed without taking lives. My father does it. You have to stop before the blood turns sweet—"

Addison shuddered and held up her hand, stopping him. Swallowing, she tried to keep the bile down that slowly crept up her throat. She couldn't stomach the idea she might actually need to feed from people.

"Will I recognize other vampires when I see them?"

"Yes. You'll know, just like I knew you were one."

With a nod, she attempted to take it all in—to understand. "Sometimes...sometimes I feel as though someone is watching me. It comes and goes. Sometimes it's strong, other times it's not. It's usually at night as though someone lurks in the shadows. I sense danger, a threat."

She glanced up at Marcus and noticed the intense, narrowed stare. "How long have you felt that?"

"Not long. Do you think it means something?"

"Vampires have heightened senses. The closer you get to ascension, the stronger they become."

"Do you think there's a problem?" Tonya asked.

Marcus pursed his lips in thought. "Maybe. But it's probably nothing."

Darkness filled the kitchen as the sun finally descended below the horizon. Marcus lifted his hand and snapped his fingers, turning on the lights and bathing the large kitchen in bright light. Marcus and Tonya both stiffened, then turned to stare toward the dining room.

Addison's hands began to shake as a feeling of dread came over her—a feeling of fear and danger. Marcus stood, slowly pushing his chair back along the tile floor. The hairs on the back of her neck stood on end as she held her breath, listening as the room filled with crackling tension.

"What's going on?" she whispered, her voice shaking slightly with nerves.

"Trouble," Marcus murmured. He turned to stare at his wife. "Stay close to me, both of you."

Tonya nodded and tugged at Addison's elbow, lifting her to shaky legs. All three watched as a tall man with long blond hair came strolling into the kitchen. His nonchalance was a stark contrast to the tension coiling his body tight, the hatred seething in his gaze. Marcus had been right. Addison knew instinctively he was a vampire—full-blooded, beautiful, and very powerful.

"Vlad," Marcus sneered.

Vlad smiled, his lips spreading into more of a sneer as his gaze wandered around the kitchen.

"Nice home," he purred and moved to stand close to Tonya. Lifting his fingers, he drew them through Tonya's hair. "You always did have excellent taste."

"Get your hands off her, Vlad," Marcus growled.

Vlad jerked his hand back with a gasp. He took a quick glance at his fingers before glaring at Marcus.

"Seems I always underestimate you and those warlock powers of yours. Making her hair burn me? Really, Marcus. Couldn't come up with anything better than that?"

"What do you want?"

Vlad inclined his head toward Addison. "Her."

Addison held her breath.

"Why?" Marcus asked.

Vlad's lips twitched. "The why is of no importance to you."

"As long as she is in my house, it is."

Addison moved to the right, pulling Tonya with her as they circled around the table, keeping Vlad on the far side.

"You have no idea, Marcus, how important she is. How desperately she's needed."

"By who?" Marcus demanded.

"Her father," Vlad replied, his lips spreading into a lustful smile.

"My what?" Addison croaked.

"You, my dear, will bring forth a new millennium. A new king." He waved his hand. "Well, at least your blood will."

She swallowed, her heart racing wildly. What did he mean by that? "My blood? What the hell are you talking about?"

"So the rumors of the blood rite are true?" Marcus asked.

"Yes. Very true. Sebastian will soon rule the vampire race, the council, and then the mortal world."

"Sebastian?" Addison's eyes widened. Sebastian was her father? The man who tried to overthrow the council was her father? "No," Addison shouted, shaking her head in denial. "I'm not that lunatic's daughter. I can't be!"

"You have no idea the power that rages through you, Addison," Vlad began. "Power passed on to you from your father, that you will give back to him on the night of your ascension. It's your blood that will raise him, that will bring our future ruler back from the dead."

Four other men came into the room. All dressed in black, all vampires, all blocking any possible exits from the room.

"Hand her over, Marcus, and we'll leave. Don't, and it will get messy."

"Fuck you, Vlad," Marcus snarled.

Vlad hissed, baring his fangs. "So be it, *warlock*."

Everything happened so fast, Addison wasn't quite sure who struck first. Marcus shouted something and sent Vlad flying across the room to land on the kitchen counter with a thud. With a gasp, she shoved Tonya between her and Marcus, protecting her. Holding up her palms, she concentrated hard on her magic, hoping she was strong enough to keep them at bay.

"*Vornak*," she murmured, creating an invisible wall between her and the three men trying to grab her.

One of the vampires growled and slapped at the wall, making everything waver like ripples in a lake. The wall began to weaken, and she changed tactics, this time striking out.

"*Minot*," she shouted, forcing the wall outward.

It slammed into the three men, shoving them onto their backs with a force strong enough to knock them out. The final man came forward as though to ram her. Addison braced herself, but a white wolf jumped from out of nowhere to land between her and the man, growling menacingly. He stopped, staring with uncertainty at the wolf, who continued to snarl. Addison was afraid to move. The wolf was obviously protecting her, but why?

"Is this yours, Marcus?" Addison whispered.

"No. That's my father's pet."

The wolf tilted his head, growling toward Marcus angrily.

"Andre doesn't like to be called a pet, Marcus."

Addison stared wide-eyed at the man who'd just spoken. He walked quickly into the room like a knight to the rescue—tall, broad, commanding. Long black hair cascaded around his shoulders, framing a face almost angelic in appearance. His eyes were a deep blue, just like Marcus's. In fact, he looked a lot like Marcus. This had to be his father…Julian. The man she'd dreamed about—the man the voice claimed needed her.

He came to a stop between the wolf and the vampire. In a soft whisper, he offered, "If I were you…I would run."

The wolf bared his fangs and made a move to attack the vampire. The vampire growled back, then disappeared into a cloud of black smoke. On the other side of the kitchen, Vlad stood, snarling at Julian. Addison watched in fascination as Julian only snorted, dismissing the threat.

"So you're sticking your nose into this, Julian?" Vlad sneered. "It wasn't enough you had to help kill the man, you think you have to protect his daughter as well?"

"Yes," Julian drawled as he slowly and deliberately moved toward the vampire. "You want her, Vlad. You have to go through me."

Addison watched as Vlad's determination wavered in the presence of Julian. It was obvious Vlad feared him as he took a step back from the dominating vampire.

"You're a fool, Julian," he snarled just before he too vanished in a puff of smoke.

"So I've been told," Julian drawled as he turned to study Addison.

She squirmed under his assessing stare. His gaze sent heat traveling to every part of her body, and her nipples hardened beneath the fabric of her top. She'd heard several things about vampires. How seductive they were, how mesmerizing, how they could hold you in a trance with their eyes. Swallowing, she watched as Julian strolled closer, his gaze never leaving hers.

He came to a stop just a couple of feet away and tilted his head. "I see a little of your father in you." She scowled, making him grin. "I take it you've heard of Sebastian?"

She nodded. "Every witch knows who Sebastian is. Word travels fast when someone tries to take over the council. He can't be my father."

Julian opened his mouth to say something, but Marcus stopped him. "How did you know?"

"Rebecca. Seems there's a rumor this was going to happen. She used some of Sebastian's things to cast a spell and find his daughter. It led me here."

"Where's Rebecca?" Tonya asked.

"I told her I would handle it and sent her back to the council."

Marcus snickered. Waving his hand, he returned the messy kitchen back to its former glory. "You mean you actually let her perform magic in your home?"

Julian shrugged one shoulder, one corner of his lips twitching in amusement. With that devilish glint in his gaze, he appeared quite adorably roguish, and her heart skipped within her chest. It was hard to believe he was Marcus's father. He looked about six years younger than his son, not older. Vampires forever remained the age they were when they were bitten. It looked as though Julian had been in his early thirties.

"She's prettier than you, Marcus, so of course I let her have her way."

"Beauty over blood," Marcus murmured. "Of course."

"Don't start you two, please," Tonya chastised as she placed her fists on her hips and stared them both down angrily. "Julian, what the hell is going on?"

With a sigh, Julian dropped into one of the chairs. His wolf, Andre, stretched out at his feet, his gold-green eyes watching Addison with interest.

"There's been a rumor for quite a while now that Sebastian's body had been prepared for a blood rite. They intend to use Addison's blood to resurrect him."

Addison scowled. "You can't be serious."

"Afraid so, *chica*," the wolf replied.

Staring wide-eyed at the wolf, she pointed her finger at the animal. "Did he just say something or am I losing my mind?"

Julian smiled. "You're not losing your mind. He can talk; it's getting him to shut up that's the challenge." The wolf huffed, his eyes narrowing. "How about taking human form, Andre, so the rest of us don't feel like fools talking to a dog?"

Slowly, the wolf morphed into a man. Tall and slim, he wore his white hair cropped short. The laugh lines surrounding his eyes crinkled as his full lips spread into a soft smile. He was the total opposite of Julian, slender where Julian was thick and muscular, light where Julian was dark. The angles of his face spoke of beauty and grace, where Julian's spoke of masculinity and raw sex appeal. The two made quite a heavenly combination.

Andre sat up, adjusting his shirt. "I'm a wolf, Julian. Say it with me... *wolf*."

Julian just snickered, his lips twitching ever so slightly. "Wolf. Dog. Same family."

"Marcus," Andre replied as he stood to his feet and stared indignantly down at the rest of them. "Your father will be the death of me."

"I have no doubt," Marcus said with a grin. "He does have a reputation for killing off his lovers. The male version of the black widow."

Fuck you, Julian mouthed, making his son grin.

"Damn it, stop!" Addison cried out in agitation. Both men turned to look at her with identical expressions of mild amusement. "My God." She sighed, staring at them. "The two of you look identical."

"Ahhh!" Marcus shouted. Turning toward the fridge, he pulled out a bottle of beer. "After that comment, I think I need a drink."

"What's wrong with looking like me?" Julian asked, his eyebrow raised. "Women love me, after all."

"Who can blame them?" Andre added.

"Absolutely," Julian agreed with a nod, his lips twitching.

Marcus snickered. "Wow, Dad. Doesn't it hurt your back when you kiss your own ass like that?"

Addison stared in exasperation. Andre chuckled. Tonya dropped her face into her hands, her shoulders shaking in silent laughter. Marcus and Julian grinned at one another like two kids. Did none of them take this seriously?

"I can't believe you," Addison growled softly, her head shaking as she stood to wave her hand in exasperation. "I was just attacked. My father is apparently Sebastian, the vampire who tried to take over the council. He wants to use my blood to resurrect himself from the sleep of the damned or death or whatever state it is he's in, and all you can do is make jokes? What if they come back? With more people?"

"Relax, Addison. They won't come back tonight."

Reaching out, Julian grasped her fingers. The warmth emanating from his touch surprised her. For some reason, she expected vampires to be cold, but he was far from cold. He tugged, gently pulling her toward him. She followed without thinking. Like a puppet controlled by her master, she did as he silently requested. With a nod, he indicated the empty chair next to him, and she sat, barely able to breathe as she stared into his eyes.

His hand kept hold of hers, his thumb gently rubbing across the backs of her fingers. Soft like a feather, they brushed across her knuckles, sending tingles of awareness up her arm. Is this what it was like to be seduced by a vampire? Is that what he was doing to her?

"I'd better not ever see you do that to my wife."

Marcus's voice seemed to come from far away, and she blinked, trying to focus on the sound instead of the heady feeling swimming through her veins. Addison turned to look at him as he leaned his hips back against the counter, beer bottle in his hand. When she looked away from Julian, some of the fogginess in her mind cleared.

"She seemed nervous," Julian replied. Addison spun back around to look at him, and he smiled softly, making her heart flutter. "I was only trying to help. I think I should take you back to Romania with me."

"What?" she breathed.

Being alone with this hunk of an immortal wasn't exactly her idea of a good plan. If she didn't get control of herself, she'd be all over him in no time at all and she had a feeling he knew that.

"Are you sure that's a good idea?" Marcus asked. "They know where you live."

"True enough," Julian murmured. "What do you suggest?"

"How about where we kept Rebecca?" Tonya offered.

"The protected dimension?" Julian sneered.

"We could cast a spell of protection. Keep her safe until her twenty-fifth birthday. The rite has to be performed during the ascension, correct? Once it's past, they will have no more use for her."

"Who protects her while I'm sleeping?"

Andre snorted. "What do I look like? Chopped liver?"

"I didn't want to speak for you, Andre," Julian replied.

"Since when?"

"This is different. Are you in?"

"Of course." Andre reached out and combed his long, slender fingers through her hair, making goose bumps rise along her flesh. She jerked her head away, causing her hair to fall from Andre's grasp. Andre smiled, then turned back to Julian. "She's too damn pretty for you to have all to yourself. Besides, she'll need someone to feed from as she turns."

Addison stiffened. "Feed from?"

"That's true," Julian replied with a nod.

"It's settled then," Marcus said with a nod.

Addison swallowed, the sudden urge to run and hide foremost in her mind. Her future, at least her immediate future anyway, had been settled without one word from her, one ounce of argument. Glancing toward Julian, she wondered how much she could really trust him. And would she really feed from Andre? The idea of drinking blood made her stomach churn.

Her life had gone from mundane to out-and-out hellish in a matter of hours.

Chapter Three

Julian struggled with his fading strength and leaned against the stone wall of the castle for support. Closing his eyes, he tried to ignore his body's need for sleep. Dawn wasn't far behind. His second dawn since the last time he'd slept.

In his mind's eye, he could see Addison. He still couldn't believe she was Sebastian's daughter. How had that coldhearted son of a bitch made something so perfect? God, she was beautiful. She looked to be about five feet six with curves that begged to be held, caressed, explored. Just thinking about it sent blood pounding through his veins.

Long auburn hair cascaded around her shoulders, curling softly on the ends. Full, kissable lips beckoned for his, while green eyes that could spark fire or were downcast in vulnerability sent tingles of heated awareness to every part of him. A woman hadn't affected him like this in a long time. It had been centuries.

He'd kept his heart hidden away for so long he was amazed he could feel anything at all other than lust. But when he looked at Addison, feelings of protectiveness and possession raced through him like a speeding bullet. He didn't know what to make of them, and frankly, they made him nervous.

Around him he could hear soft voices as Andre, Marcus, and Tonya explained the castle and grounds to Addison. The stone structure resided in the witch's protected dimension stationed just outside the realm of the mortal world. They could hide here in relative safety. Until their presence was discovered. Everyone knew of his aversion to magic, so hopefully the vampires after Addison would think of this as the last place he'd be. As time drew closer to her twenty-fifth birthday, Sebastian's followers would become more desperate.

A blood rite may or may not kill Addison. A lot of it would depend on her inner strength as well as Sebastian's. The weaker he was, the more blood they would need from Addison.

His fingers clenched at his sides as he imagined them draining Addison. He couldn't let that happen.

"How long has it been since you've slept, Julian?" Marcus asked, concern lacing his son's voice.

Without opening his eyes, he replied, "Almost thirty-six hours."

"That can't be good for you."

Tonya's soft voice came from beside him, and he turned his head slightly in her direction. Opening his gaze, he smiled at her. "I'll be fine once I get some sleep."

"Do that now, Julian," his son ordered in his usual commanding tone. Julian recognized it as a trait Marcus had inherited from him. "I'll set something up for you in the basement, away from the light."

"I hate basements," he murmured.

Pushing away from the wall, he locked gazes with Addison. She stood just a few feet away, studying him. He could see the uncertainty in her eyes, the weariness in her stance. She had a rough time ahead of her. His stomach tightened as he thought of the danger she was in—the danger they were all in.

She hugged her sweater closer to her chest as though to ward off the chill. Was she cold? For some reason he had the desire to enfold her in his arms and warm her, comfort her. He needed sleep first, though; his body would shut down without it. He would have to leave the comforting to Andre for now. He knew his friend would take care of her.

He moved forward, coming to a stop next to Addison. He brushed her cheek with the backs of his fingers, allowing the heat from her soft flesh to warm them. As he watched, her tongue flicked out to lick her lips, and a rosy flush moved over her face. Inwardly, he groaned at what that tiny movement did to his libido. Even as tired as he was, he wanted to kiss her, taste her, see if her lips were as soft as they looked.

"Andre will take care of you until I wake." Turning to his son, he added, "She seems cold; see if you can get it a little warmer in here for her."

Marcus nodded, then turned to lead Julian to the basement.

Addison watched him go with a frown. His touch had made her insides quiver. Even now, she could still feel the heat of his hand, still smell his musky scent. Was it lust? Was it his vampire magnetism? Her gaze wandered down his wide back, trim waist, and firm ass. His black hair hung halfway down his back, the long strands reflecting the soft light of the room. She sighed, pursing her lips in thought. It was definitely magnetism, but more of the lustful kind.

Her mother had kept her sequestered, sheltered, and she knew very little about her father's race. It was only during the months before her death that her mother had admitted her father was a vampire. She'd fluctuated between terror and anger ever since. Meeting Julian hadn't really helped much. Now she was not only terrified of turning, but of what her body felt when he was near—of the control he obviously had over her, and it took nothing more than a stare.

As Julian disappeared down the hall, her gaze shifted to Andre. What exactly was he to Julian? A friend? Lover? In her mind, she tried to imagine the two of them kissing. Would Julian be the dominant one? More than likely so. Andre seemed more charming and almost boyish than dominant. That didn't mean he didn't exude his own unusual sex appeal. Quite the contrary.

Although not as muscular, Andre had the body of a runner—tall and lean. His gaze was sharp as a tack, never missing anything as he scanned the area around him, or when he looked at her, which he did now. Leaning against the stone wall, he crossed his arms over his chest and smiled knowingly. Her stomach flipped at how that smile transformed his face. How strange was it to be attracted to two men so totally opposite?

Shaking off her very inappropriate thoughts, she moved to the massive stone fireplace. With a wave of her hand, she had a fire blazing, warming her chilled flesh. With a sigh, she stepped back and dropped onto the sofa, her gaze glued to the red and gold flames licking at the air.

Andre grabbed the off-white cashmere throw from the corner of the couch and covered her legs. "I'm going to go prowl the grounds. I'll be back shortly. Why don't you try to get some sleep as well? Julian will be up in a few hours, and I'm sure he'll want to talk with you."

Addison nodded and stretched out along the soft leather. Now that things were quiet and she felt relatively safe, she could admit to the fatigue draining her. This sluggish feeling during the day happened more and more as she got closer to her birthday. When the sun went down was when she felt more rejuvenated, more alive.

With a soft smile, Andre adjusted the blanket, then gently brushed the hair from her brow. His touch singed her skin, made her tingle, and she tugged at the blanket, pulling it closer to her chin.

"Tonya and Marcus will be here until I return, so if you need anything, call out for them."

Addison nodded. With a tap to her nose, Andre turned and leaned forward. As he did, his body began to morph into the form of the white wolf. His front paws hit the ground and he leaped out the open French doors and onto the grounds. To see him do that was amazing, and she kept her gaze on his sleek, furry form as he roamed the gardens beyond until he disappeared from view.

Tonya stood next to the fireplace, watching her with concern. "Are you okay?"

"I've been better," she murmured. "I'm just so tired."

"You've been up almost all night. It's understandable."

"Lately, I'm always tired during the day no matter how much sleep I get the night before. Do you think that means anything?"

"I don't know. Julian will, though."

Julian.

Addison's gaze moved to the flames as she thought about the gorgeous vampire. Was he sleeping? Rejuvenating? Had he been experiencing the same dreams she had?

Slowly, her eyes grew heavy and the flames blurred as she fell off to sleep, her thoughts on Julian and Andre.

Mist surrounded her, called to her as she strolled through the darkened gardens. Moonlight cut a streak of light through the mist, highlighting the path in front of her. The scent of jasmine filled the cool air and she breathed deeply of its heady fragrance.

Ahead of her a form appeared. It was a wolf, its white fur ruffling in the night breeze, its eyes aglow with hunger and passion. Behind the wolf stood Julian, his dark hair framing his face, his shirt open and showing off his smooth, hard chest. He too looked at her with desire. Dark and sultry, his stare made her body tremble.

The wolf stepped forward, morphing into Andre as he got closer. He grasped her fingers, bringing them to his lips and placing a soft kiss against her knuckles that sent tingles up her arm. With a devilish smile, he moved behind her and placed a teasing kiss just below her ear. The butterflies in her stomach went wild.

Her stare moved to Julian as he strolled forward, his hot, searing gaze boring into hers. Her heart began to race wildly as he stepped closer, dwarfing her with his massive frame. Reaching out, he cupped the side of her face, his touch gentle and warm. Her reaction to both men scared her, confused her. She didn't understand it, but knew she wanted them both beyond reason—knew she needed them.

Without warning, their warmth was gone and she was left alone in the dark. Danger swarmed around her; she could feel its icy presence getting closer, threatening her, suffocating her.

She took a step back, away from the swirling mist and the unknown lurking within its depths. A form appeared within the mist, sending a tremor of apprehension up her spine. Tall and broad, he moved toward her from the fog, the wind blowing the cloak around his shoulders. In his hand was a cane; the red eyes of the serpent covering the tip glistened in the moonlight as though to send a warning. Evil surrounded him like a shroud, threatening to overwhelm her.

Tightening her spine, she stood her ground, refusing to be afraid.

"My child," he murmured as he came forward, the dark form taking shape.

Long white hair surrounded his shoulders, his eyes glistening with evil.

"I'm not your child," she snapped. "I'm not helping you."

He hissed, baring his vampire fangs. "You don't have any choice in the matter. This is why I impregnated your mother. This is why you exist, Addison. As my link to life."

"Screw you," *she snarled, backing away.*

He laughed, low, deep, sadistically. She covered her ears, trying to drown out the sound, to make it go away, but it grew louder, surrounding her, trying to penetrate her. Scrunching her eyes tightly closed, she tried to imagine home, tried to bring herself out of the dream.

"Julian," she whispered. "Andre."

His laughter turned to an angry roar, shaking the very ground beneath her feet, and she screamed.

Addison awoke with a start, her eyes darting around the room checking all the darkened corners, the hall just beyond the open doors. She was alone except for the white wolf lounging on the other end of the long sofa, his head resting on her calf. The red embers from the fire cast an orange glow against his fur. With a sigh, she realized it had all been a dream.

Andre's ear jerked and he lifted his head, staring at her. Opening his mouth, he yawned, making her smile.

"Sleep well, Andre?" she asked.

She would swear he made a face before morphing back to his human form. His head rested just at her hip, his white hair perfect, his smile devilish.

"Nice spot to find myself," he said with a grin as he leaned down to place a kiss on her hip through the blanket.

Ignoring the heat traveling up her thigh, she asked, "I initially thought you were a werewolf, but you're not, are you?"

"No. Shape-shifter."

"Can you change into anything else?"

"No. Just the wolf."

"How long have you known Julian?"

He rested his chin on her hip, studying her, a slight grin tugging at his lips. "Are we playing twenty questions? If so, when is it my turn?"

She snickered, rising to her elbow, then shrugged one shoulder. "I just wanted to know about the men assigned to protect me. I've spent most of my life on a farm in a small Midwestern town, Andre. I don't know a lot about the world or the various species that occupy it. I didn't even know until a few months ago that my father was a vampire."

He gave her thigh a soft pat and sat up, leaning his back against the opposite armrest. Outside the sky was still light, though tinges of red and gold lined the horizon. Sunset would be on them soon and Julian would be awake. Sitting up as well, she turned to face Andre.

"Ask me anything, Addy. I'm an open book."

"Addy?" she asked. No one had ever shortened her name before, and she found she actually liked it.

"Don't like it?" he asked. "Would you prefer Add?"

She scrunched her nose. "Addy's good."

With a chuckle, Andre adjusted his white shirt, allowing her a glimpse of the white hair covering his chest. When she raised her eyes back to his face, she noticed with embarrassment he'd seen where she'd been staring. Heat flooded her face and she glanced down, fiddling with the blanket still covering her legs.

"Are you and Julian lovers?"

"Depends on your interpretation of lovers."

She glanced up at him. "Do you have sex with each other?"

"No."

She nodded, nervously licking her lips.

"We share women, and we have been known to touch and kiss each other while making love to a woman, but I have never fucked him." He grinned. "Nor has he me, just in case you were thinking of asking."

Addison shrugged, her embarrassment growing. "Marcus made that comment about Julian killing his lovers and…"

"Julian has had male lovers. So have I. But that's not what our relationship is. We're very good friends. I suppose you could say I'm his servant."

"Servant?" she asked, frowning.

"Yes. I've been with Julian many years. He saved me as a child, so I felt indebted to him. We grew to be very close. He's a good man…deep down." He grinned. "*Way* deep down."

Addison smiled, but it quickly faded. "Has he killed his past lovers?"

Andre's lips twitched in amusement. "You'll have to learn to take what Marcus says about Julian with a grain of salt. He loves to goad his father. Julian has only killed one lover. He was trying to kill Julian's son. He didn't have a choice."

"Yeah, I've noticed how the two of them"—Addison raised her hands and arched the first two fingers on each hand, emphasizing her next words—"pick at each other."

"Those two have a very strange relationship, but they're trying. Julian loved Marcus's mother very much, and she broke his heart. I'm not sure he's ever been the same."

"Andre," Julian growled from the far side of the room.

He stood in the shadows, careful to keep his feet on the outside of the last rays of light streaking across the hardwood floors. Addison couldn't take her eyes off him. He wore all black—black trousers, black turtleneck, black shoes. His eyes, though, shone the most intense shade of blue, standing out in stark contrast to the black of his hair and lashes.

"She asked a question, I answered it. Get over it."

Julian rolled his eyes. "Did you sleep well, Addison?"

"I suppose." She frowned, watching him as he followed the shadow across the room. Was he always so gruff? So cold? "What did my father look like?" she asked as her thoughts traveled back to the dream and the man in it.

"He was tall, white hair like Andre, broad like me. Why?"

"I dreamed of him," she whispered. "He said I was his link to life."

Julian and Andre shared a look that made her nervous.

Andre turned back to her. Reaching out, he rubbed at her calf. "It was probably just a bad dream brought on by what we talked about yesterday. Nothing more."

"Then how did I know what he looked like?"

"Maybe you have a little psychic ability. It's not unheard of among witches," Julian offered as he moved farther into the room, following the fading sunlight.

"Maybe," she mumbled, but doubted it.

She'd never had that ability before. Only the most powerful of witches were able to catch glimpses of the future. Powerful was certainly not how she would describe herself. Shy, quiet, reserved was more her style. Her mother had been so protective of her growing up. Was it because she knew what would happen? Had she known what her father had in mind for her?

"Are you hungry, Addison?"

She glanced up at Andre and frowned. Hungry? No, she wasn't hungry. Matter of fact, she couldn't remember the last time she ate and her frown deepened. "I, ah…I haven't been hungry in a while, actually."

"How long has it been since you've eaten?" Julian asked as he leaned casually against the edge of the fireplace.

"I'm not sure. Day before yesterday, maybe."

Andre raised one eyebrow. "And you're still not hungry?"

She shook her head, her stomach knotting in apprehension.

"Her body is starting the process," Julian explained. "She'll eat very little over the next couple of weeks, if anything at all."

"Won't that make me sick?"

"No. Your body's dying, Addison."

She scowled at his cold attitude. "You have one hell of a bedside manner, do you know that?"

He shrugged. "Would you prefer changing then, as opposed to dying?"

Pushing away from the fireplace, he walked toward her. With one hand on the armrest behind her and the other on the back of the sofa, he leaned down, putting his nose close to hers. His gaze held hers captive as she pressed back against the armrest to get as much distance between them as possible. This close, she could see tiny flecks of lighter blue around his pupils. The smell of musk and mint invaded her nose, making her inhale deeper, both to capture more of the scent as well as calm her nerves.

"You are dying, Addison, and you will become another member of the undead. Face it. It's how you choose to use your new abilities that I'm curious to see. Will you be your own person or will you turn out like your father?"

"I don't even know my father," she snarled.

"It's probably best you don't. That will make your killing him so much easier for you."

She stopped breathing. "What?"

"If you're to survive, that's what you'll have to do. If they get you and take you to him on the night of your ascension, it's you or him. If he survives, it will be a war unlike any mortals have ever seen."

"And if I survive?" she demanded.

"That remains to be seen."

Chapter Four

"Where's Addison?" Andre asked.

He didn't have to look up from cutting the vegetables to know Julian had entered the kitchen. They'd been friends long enough he could sense when he was close by. His heightened senses picked up his scent and his nostrils flared.

"She's on the patio, just staring at the moon."

Picking up a knife, Julian jabbed it into the wooden slab of the cutting table. Andre looked up and didn't miss the frown of apprehension across his friend's brow. He had a feeling this wasn't going to be easy. He was just as attracted to Addison as Julian was, which would probably not play out well for any of them.

"You don't think you were a little harsh with her earlier? I really didn't think you'd tell her on the first day she would have to kill her own father."

Julian toyed with the knife, twirling the tip into the wood. "It's best she know up front what's about to happen."

"She's already showing signs of change. She slept all day and awoke at sunset."

Julian shrugged, his troubled gaze glued to the knife. "She could have just been tired."

"If she doesn't become a full vampire, they'll have to kill her to get enough of her blood. Would that bother you?"

Julian scowled at him through his lashes. "I'm not having this discussion with you, Andre."

"What discussion?"

"The discussion where you dig and try to find out what my feelings are."

"Fine." Andre sighed, moving his attention back to the vegetables he was chopping for dinner. Julian might not need to eat, but he did. "Grab me a cup of coffee," he demanded angrily.

"Sure, Andre. You want it black or a with a couple of cubes of kiss-my-ass?" Julian replied, sarcasm dripping from his voice.

"Sorry," Andre said as he grinned up at him. "Didn't mean to come across quite so bossy. What's with you tonight? You're being more of an ass than usual."

"I just have a bad feeling."

Julian poured coffee into a cup and set it on the counter next to him. Reaching for the steaming cup, Andre caught a glimpse of Addison as she slowly strolled into the room from the open patio doors. Her jeans and shirt looked a little rumpled from having been slept in, and her hair began to form ringlet curls from the cool night air. With her porcelain skin and pouty lips, she looked like a doll. So perfect. If she had any idea what he wanted to do to her right now, she'd run screaming.

His cock thickened in his pants and he shifted slightly, trying to find a more comfortable stance. As he did, he studied his friend. Hunger lit up his blue eyes as he stared at Addison. Andre knew that look. He wanted her too.

He took a sip of his coffee, before quickly setting the cup down and resuming cutting the vegetables again—anything to distract him so he could get his cock back under control.

"You're cooking?" she asked as she came to stand on the other side of the small island.

He glanced up at her and smiled. "Yes. I'm not like you, sweetheart. I have to eat." The knife missed the onions, sinking into his finger with a sharp burn. "Son of a bitch," he hissed, pulling his hand away from the cutting board to examine how deep the cut went.

As though in a trance, Addison watched the blood spill from the deep cut on Andre's finger. Her heart pounded wildly and a hunger formed deep in her gut, spreading throughout her body. Trembling fingers gripped the edge of the island and she licked her lips. A sudden and overwhelming desire to lick that blood surged through her with a force that almost brought her to her knees.

"Let me see that," Julian commanded as he stepped forward and took Andre's hand in his, bringing it to his lips.

"Wait." Andre caught Julian's wrist with his uninjured hand, stopping him. "Addison?" he asked, watching her closely.

Addison couldn't take her gaze off his hand and the blood sliding down his arm. She shook her head, refusing to accept what was happening. She couldn't want that. No. Her stomach lurched and she ran from the room back to the patio, gulping in the cool night air.

No. This can't be happening.

"Addison," Julian said from behind her, his voice soft and soothing.

She took two deep breaths, trying to control the hunger gnawing at her insides like blades.

"I can't do it," she whispered, tears of anger streaming down her face. "I don't want to become like you."

"You don't have a choice."

"I can fight it," she argued with growing determination, swiping away the tears streaming down her cheeks. "I know I can fight it."

"For a time, maybe, but eventually it will take over. It will eat you alive until there's nothing left but a hunger you can't control. Trust me, Addison. You don't want that to happen."

She sobbed, her shoulders shaking uncontrollably as sorrow filled her soul. Her life as she knew it was over. No more days at the lake, no more sunshine, no more blue sky. She would become a beast. A monster. A killer.

"I can teach you, Addison," Julian whispered, and her stomach jerked at the sound of his deep, husky voice and the effect it had on her. "I can help you control it. I can teach you to feed without taking a life."

Andre stepped in front of her, his hand dripping blood. Her gaze dropped to the red liquid, and the hunger began again—painful, overwhelming. She gasped, her breathing harsh and short. With a groan, she closed her eyes, shaking her head in denial, trying to ignore the sharp tightening of her stomach.

"No…no."

Julian moved to stand next to Andre. Taking Andre's hand, Julian lifted his finger to his lips and drew it into his mouth. She watched in growing fascination as Julian sucked the blood from Andre's finger. He closed his eyes, sighing as his tongue licked away the final drops.

Without warning, Julian gripped the back of her head and tugged her to him. Her lips parted in a soft gasp as she tried to pull away, but he held her tight and planted his mouth across hers, his tongue seeking entrance past the slight part in her lips. The spicy taste of blood lingered in his mouth and she moaned, thrusting her tongue inside to seek more of the taste. It wasn't gentle. It was rough, wild, hungry. She needed that taste like she needed air to breathe and the very idea sent anger coursing through her with a vengeance.

Julian pulled away and she whimpered, wanting desperately to have more. Fisting her fingers into his shirt, she tried to pull him back, unable to think of anything other than getting more of that taste. Fangs descended into place and she scraped her tongue across them.

"Deep breaths," he whispered, pulling back against her hold but not breaking it. "Breathe, Addison."

Closing her eyes, she tried to concentrate on the deep rumble of his voice as she drew in two deep breaths, then another. Slowly, she began to settle down, and a warm peace settled in her chest.

"That came on much sooner than I expected," Andre murmured, his voice laced with concern.

"There's more blood on his finger." Julian spoke softly, soothingly. "I want you to lick it off…slowly."

She shook her head, wanting to refuse, but at the same time, needing that taste again. He turned her so she faced Andre. Julian moved behind her, his hands holding her wrists at her sides, his lips close to her ear. He held her steady, gave her strength and comfort.

With a look of total understanding and trust, Andre placed his finger at her lips. The metallic scent of blood filled her senses and burned through her like lightning. Her nostrils flared. Fighting hard against the desire to suck his finger into her mouth, she licked her tongue along the length of his digit, savoring the spicy taste.

"That's it, baby," Julian whispered. "You control the hunger. You must always control it."

She hissed. "I can't. I…"

"Shhh," Julian whispered.

Andre squeezed his finger, forcing more blood from the wound. Addison swallowed as her fangs again dipped into place. Tears streamed down her cheeks as she stared at Andre's finger. "I don't want to hurt you."

"I trust you, Addy," he whispered softly. "Julian will help you. Listen to him. Trust him."

"Lick his finger, baby…slowly."

Letting Julian's deep voice resonate through her, she leaned forward slightly and licked her tongue up Andre's finger. The warm, spicy taste of blood filled her mouth, but instead of lessening the hunger, it seemed to increase it. Pain spread through her limbs. Pain mixed with euphoria as his blood mingled with her own.

Andre pressed his finger into her mouth and she sucked, wildly at first, hungrily. She struggled to break free of Julian's grip, but he held her still, immobile.

"It tastes spicy now, warm…but eventually it will turn sweet. When it does, that means death for the victim. It's hard to resist," Julian murmured. "Hard to stop once you get that first taste of sweetness. It's best you never taste it."

Images of bloody necks ripped open and wild-eyed monsters made her whole body tremble, and she jerked her head to the side, forcing herself to let go of Andre's finger. Sobs racked her frame as Julian wrapped his arms around her from behind, holding her as she cried out her grief, her pain.

"You did good, Addy," Andre whispered, placing a soft kiss on her brow. "It gets easier, I promise."

* * *

"Try some of this, it might help."

Addison stared up at Andre with a frown. Her stomach still rumbled and the acrid taste of blood still filled her mouth. The hunger, that gnawing hunger still ate away at her insides. Would she ever be free of it?

Her gaze dropped to the bowl of soup he set before her and her nose wrinkled.

"You haven't completely turned yet. It might help to settle your stomach," Julian offered.

What the hell? What could it hurt? It might at least get rid of this taste. Lifting the spoon, she brought a bite to her mouth but tasted nothing. It was like eating cardboard. With a grimace, she spit it back out into her napkin.

"I know I'm not the greatest cook in the world, but damn," Andre teased.

Wiping her mouth, she stared down at her shaking hands. Her head snapped up, her gaze moving from the knowing look on Julian's face to the raised eyebrow of Andre.

"The soup tasted like cardboard, Andre. I'm so sorry," she whispered.

"It's expected, although it's happening surprisingly fast. Are you sure you have your birthday right?" Julian asked.

"Of course," she snapped, glancing toward Julian and his narrowed stare. He studied her in a way that made her nervous, as though he was reading her thoughts, trying to determine if she were lying or not. "What?"

"I believe you're going to be a full vampire. You can't eat food, at all."

Her lower lip began to tremble and she swallowed down a lump the size of a baseball. "I pray you're wrong," she whispered, her voice shaky.

"I pray I'm not." He leaned forward slightly, his voice low and ominous as he spoke. "I believe it's the only way you'll survive your father's blood rite."

Chapter Five

Sitting outside on the garden bench, Addison tried to keep the racking sobs shaking her body as silent as possible. Surely he was wrong. He had to be wrong.

She didn't want to be a vampire. She could live with being a half-breed. She would rather be a half-breed. At least then she would still be able to eat the food she enjoyed, drink a glass of wine, and maybe even get drunk. God, what she wouldn't give to be able to get drunk right now.

Angrily wiping at the tears streaming down her cheeks, she glanced up at the full moon lighting the garden. Why couldn't she stop fucking crying? She was stronger than this; what the hell was wrong with her?

The scent of jasmine filled the air, along with rose and honeysuckle. It was so beautiful here, but she couldn't enjoy it. All she could think about was how her life was changing.

To her left, Andre emerged in the form of the wolf. He sat at her feet, watching her. Sniffing, she rested her hand on his head, running her fingers through his soft white fur.

"I don't want to be a monster, Andre," she whispered, her voice breaking on a sob.

Turning his head, Andre licked at her palm and she smiled softly. Andre was so different from Julian. The dominating vampire scared her because of his dangerous reputation as well as his raw sex appeal. Addison was by no means a cowering virgin, but Julian sent her senses into a tailspin. Add to Julian Andre's more subtle allure and she was a goner.

She'd never been attracted to two men at once. Not ever. She didn't have a clue how to handle it or if she even *should* handle it. For all she knew, they were here to protect her and nothing more. But even now as she stared into Andre's soft eyes, she couldn't stop thinking about Julian's kiss—about how his lips had felt against hers, and some small part of her wondered if Andre could kiss just as well.

With a sigh, she glanced back up at the sky and the thin clouds slowly moving across the moon.

"Are we going to stay here the whole time or can we leave?" she asked Andre, but it was another, darker voice that answered her.

"We will leave at some point," Julian replied from behind her.

Addison jumped and turned to watch as he sauntered forward and sat beside her on the bench.

"I will need to feed," Julian said.

Addison shuddered.

"And so will you."

Her eyes narrowed. "What?"

"I want to train you on Andre first, but you can't feed from him too much or you'll kill him."

"No," she argued, shaking her head. "I'm not ready for this."

"You don't have a choice, Addison. Andre is not unfamiliar with this. I've fed from him before."

"Oh, well then," she replied sarcastically. "Set him on a silver platter and bring him forth."

Andre snickered, then returned to human form. Crossing his legs, he remained on the grass, his expression one of amusement and understanding. "You have to learn control, Addy. Besides, I somewhat enjoy it. It can be rather arousing."

"You can't be serious. Doesn't it hurt?"

"Not if you do it right," Julian replied. "And at the right time."

"And when is the right time?"

"Usually as they climax."

She swallowed, glancing sideways toward Julian as a slight tremor ran through her body. Suddenly, he sat way too close. Her nostrils flared, picking up his musky scent mingling with the floral scent of the garden.

"So you feed during sex?" she murmured.

"Usually, yes. It's the most pleasurable for the victim, and they never remember the next day, and if they do, they just think it was part of the sex," Julian answered.

"So when I feed from Andre will we be having sex?"

"If that is what you wish," Julian said softly, his deep voice sending tingles down her spine.

Was it what she wished? Her heightened senses had begun to pick up on things she wasn't quite ready to deal with—Andre's arousal, Julian's scent and warmth, the sound of their breathing as they watched her, studied her.

Everything she felt, smelled, heard was magnified—heightened.

"When will we do this?" she asked breathlessly.

"The sooner the better. Your reaction to the sight of Andre's blood earlier indicates you're closer to ascension than we originally thought. You need to learn control before you fully turn. At that point it will be more difficult if you don't already have a slight handle on it."

Andre slipped his hand up her calf, caressing her skin with featherlight strokes of his fingers. Her flesh heated beneath his touch and the heat shining in his gaze, so she shifted her stare to his white hair, studying how the moonlight highlighted the strands. Anything to take her mind off the erotic sensations coursing through her.

Is this what it would be like whenever she was around an aroused male? Or was it her own heightened arousal making her shudder?

"Why don't you go for a swim in the pool?" Andre suggested. "The water is warm, the moonlight beautiful. It will relax you."

Addison sighed. "I'm not sure there's much of anything that will relax me at the moment. But a swim does sound nice." She glanced down at herself. "I don't have any other clothes."

Julian snickered. "Did you forget you're a witch?"

Addison froze, then half chuckled. "I guess I did. Shows just how frazzled I am at the moment."

She closed her eyes against the warming sensation traveling up her leg where Andre continued to massage.

"I think I will go for that swim," she murmured. She needed to get away from them for a minute and cool her head as well as her ardor. "Where's the pool?"

"Follow the path, then go right when it forks," Julian said with a nod. "The pool is down by the lake. There are towels in the stone cavern, and also a hot tub tucked inside."

"We'll give you as much privacy as we can, but I'm afraid we can't leave you completely alone, just in case they know we're here."

"Great," she grumbled.

Her stomach started fluttering with nerves at the thought of swimming in front of them. She would prefer to swim naked, but did she dare with them so close? Her nipples tingled as erotic thoughts began to race through her mind. Her thoughts mingled with the bombardment of sensations she was already experiencing, making her break into a sweat.

Standing abruptly, she swallowed down her own desire. Andre's hand fell from her calf while Julian watched her with a knowing look that made her want to scream. She needed that swim. Naked or not, she needed to feel cool water against her heating body before she did something really stupid.

"I'm going to go for that swim," she mumbled, then turned to head down the path but threw over her shoulder as an afterthought, "but at least turn your backs as I undress."

"Right," Andre murmured, watching her go.

Julian bit back a grin. He had to admit he was just as anxious to see the body beneath her conservative clothes as Andre appeared to be. Standing, he motioned for his friend to follow him as they made their way to the pool. They couldn't afford to leave her alone. Even here in the protected dimension, they weren't truly safe.

Just ahead of them, he caught a glimpse of her as she stepped through the wrought iron gate surrounding the pool. The sound of the twelve-foot waterfall that emptied into the deep end of the pool carried across the breeze. Behind it was the rock grotto, which hid the towels and hot tub.

He and Andre followed through the gate and watched as she slowly stripped off her clothes. One by one, her garments fell to the ground exposing her smooth skin and lean body. The moonlight reflected off the flesh of her hips and he imagined stroking that gentle slope as his hand glided over her ass, then between her legs to stroke her pussy.

His cock hardened and he shifted to ease some of the pressure. Unfortunately, it did nothing to help. At least her back was to them and he didn't have to suffer through staring at her breasts. Even through her clothes earlier, he could tell they were the perfect size. High and firm, they would be just the right fit for his palms.

He swallowed as she bent one leg, allowing the toes of her other foot to dip into the water. Goose bumps rose along the flesh of her back as a warm breeze blew, ruffling her hair. With a shiver, she crossed her arms over her chest and glanced up at the cloudless sky before taking a deep breath and jumping into the water.

She remained under for several seconds and Julian walked closer to the edge, his gaze finding her quickly as she swam along the bottom. Her hair floated around her like a cloud as she moved through the water and he smiled.

"This is going to be a long fucking night," Andre grumbled in French as he came to stand beside him.

Julian glanced over at his friend, then lower toward his hard cock straining behind the zipper of his pants. "Perhaps you should take care of that before she sees you," Julian suggested.

Andre snorted, dropping his gaze to stare at Julian's cock, which was just as hard as Andre's. "Like you're any better off. Perhaps we should reconsider the no sex with each other rule."

"Are you making a pass at me, Andre?" he asked, although his gaze remained on Addison as she sliced through the water to the surface.

Her hands brushed the water from her eyes and off her forehead. It was the sexiest thing he'd seen in a long damn time.

"I would prefer Addison, but at the moment, I would take you in a pinch," Andre murmured.

Addison turned to stare at them, and Julian had to remind himself to breathe. He took a deep breath and let it out slowly. "Enjoying the water?"

"Enjoying the view?" she countered.

Julian smiled. "I think if you looked at us hard enough, the answer to that would be obvious."

Her gaze dropped to his cock, then moved to Andre's. A slight flush covered her cheeks, barely visible in the moonlight. "It appears that you are," she grumbled.

Andre gave her a lopsided grin. "Most women would be flattered."

"So. Doesn't mean I am."

She bit at her lower lip, watching them both warily.

"We won't bite you, Addy," Andre said, then grinned wickedly. "Well, at least I won't," he added, nodding toward Julian.

"Vampires don't normally feed off each other. Doesn't mean I won't bite, though."

He winked, enjoying the way Addison's eyes widened slightly as desire began to darken the color. She was so damn pretty. Too pretty, and he couldn't stop looking at her, thinking about touching her, tasting her. He hadn't been this attracted to a woman in years. Centuries.

Truthfully, women had begun to bore him. They'd lost their appeal, but suddenly, looking at Addison, he found himself lusting after her like a teenager. The fact he could pick up on her desire as well only intensified his own, making his balls incredibly uncomfortable. If this kept up, he'd either have to fuck her or take Andre up on his suggestion. It wouldn't be the first time he'd had a male lover.

He didn't need this, nor did he want it. As much as he hated to admit it, his heart still belonged to Kayla. He hadn't been able to let go—of her or the hurt—when she couldn't bring herself to accept his world.

Sex had been reduced to fucking for him. There was no emotional connection, no love. Nothing. At times, he felt dead inside and it had been that way for a long time. That is, until he looked at Addison. Her vulnerability, her innocence, her beauty…they all sparked a small piece of him to life, touched a part of his soul he thought long dead.

Without even thinking about it, he crossed his arms and gripped the bottom edges of his shirt, then tugged it over his head. His gaze remained locked with Addison's. She stared at his chest, desire mingling with the confusion and uncertainty swimming in the depths of her sparkling eyes. He could feel her lust. Hear her blood coursing through her veins. God, he could even smell her and his hands began to tremble with the need to touch her, explore her curves.

Andre followed Julian's lead, throwing his shirt to one of the chairs a few feet away. His friend quickly removed his pants and shoes, then jumped into the water with a splash. Addison squealed, turning her head to the side.

Julian took his time, standing still until her gaze moved back to him.

Addison couldn't help but stare at Julian. His hair hung around his shoulders, the moonlight reflecting off the black and making his tan skin shimmer. Muscles flexed as he moved, and she swallowed at the strength he exuded. The man could easily crush her.

He looked dangerous and incredibly seductive. Her pussy was getting wet just looking at him. His eyes practically glowed with lust, making her skin tingle. Even the warm water did nothing to cool her quickly rising passion.

Was it her imagination or did she truly feel his desire for her? She could hear the beat of three hearts, her own as well as theirs, pounding through her ears, and she swallowed with anxiety. The feeling was overwhelming, almost scary but unbelievably erotic at the same time.

Andre surfaced behind her and moved to press his chest to her back. His presence was far from soothing as his hands rested gently at her hips, holding her still against him. His hard cock pressed into the small of her back and her stomach tensed. Why couldn't she contest this? Why was she waiting here, doing nothing?

"He looks magnificent, doesn't he?" Andre whispered in her ear, and she nodded without thinking.

Julian did indeed look magnificent and she couldn't stop staring as his fingers unzipped his slacks, freeing his long, thick, thoroughly glorious cock.

Wow. Oh wow.

Her pussy clenched at the thought of that shaft buried deep inside her, the feel of those arms wrapped around her and those luscious lips molded to hers. He pushed his pants down, exposing thick, muscular thighs that made her mouth water.

Vampires kept the form they had when they were changed. Vaguely, she wondered what he did all those years ago. Who was he?

"How old are you, Julian?" she asked, her voice sounding breathless even to her own ears.

"Well over eight hundred years," he replied softly, then moved to sit on the edge of the pool, his lower legs dangling in the water. "The exact number I'm not sure of."

"Lost count?"

He shrugged. "Didn't care anymore."

His gaze darkened, making her shiver in anticipation. Andre swayed against her, his fingers sensually massaging her hips, and she felt herself sagging into him, her legs turning to mush.

"I think we could think of so many things other than age to talk about," Julian murmured, his voice deep and sultry, almost hypnotic. "Don't you?"

"Like what?" she whispered, unsure what was happening to her.

Her nipples beaded as the water lapped around them, making them ache and tingle. Her stomach knotted and her pussy leaked cream; she could feel it on the insides of her thighs as Andre gently pushed her closer to the dark angel before her.

"Like sex."

She swallowed as those feelings of hunger began to build inside her. Hunger not only for that glorious cock she was almost eye level with, but for blood. She licked her lips.

"What if I need to...?" She swallowed again, barely able to say the words past the growing lump in her throat. "To feed?"

"I'll help you through it, Addison."

She nodded, for some reason trusting him.

"You can feed from me," Andre whispered. His lips softly nipped at the sensitive flesh below her ear and she shivered. "You can feed from me while Julian and I show you pleasure you only dreamed of before."

His hand slid around to the front, then lower, brushing over her mound. Her head fell back and her legs spread below the water. The rush of warm pool water joined his fingers as he fondled her pussy, just barely touching her.

"You shave," he whispered, his voice portraying his approval.

"Yes," she mumbled, opening her eyes to look at Julian.

He watched them quietly, his gaze dark, his eyes slightly narrowed. His palm moved to cup his cock, his fingers circling the thick rod at the base, and she was barely able to contain a moan of pleasure at the sight of him. Andre's fingers separated her labia, teasing the wet opening to her pussy. She bit down, drawing blood from her lower lip.

The taste filled her mouth and she drew in a deep, shuddering breath. The hunger built deep in her stomach, matching the rise of her desire. Scents and sounds surrounding her began to intensify, invading her senses and pushing her to a state of sensory overload. She could even detect Julian's and Andre's scents. They were so distinct, so different, she could pick them out without any trouble.

A drop of precum dotted the head of Julian's shaft, and he brushed his thumb across it, smearing it around the head. Her nostrils flared as the musky scent washed over her. Andre's lips continued to nibble at her neck, making her dizzy and wanton.

Was Julian just going to sit there or was he going to join in?

"Do you just watch?" she asked, fighting the rising desire to drink from Andre again.

She fought for control of her desire; she could feel it building higher, fighting to take her over. She could hardly breathe or think as Julian slid into the pool. The water sloshed around his waist as he moved forward, ever closer to her and Andre.

"In the beginning," he explained as his hand came up to cup her cheek.

His thumb brushed along her jaw and then her lower lip. Her mouth parted, and her tongue flicked out to lick at it. She savored the salty taste, the warm, musky smell of his flesh.

"The hunger will come from nowhere and everywhere. The scent of blood, the sight of it, even the thought of it will bring it on. Arousal will intensify it, yours as well as your mates'."

Her lower lip trembled as her desires began to rise ever higher. Her gaze dropped to his neck, where his pulse beat a strong, steady rhythm. "How can I control it? Even now, I need it so bad, I hurt."

Andre sucked at her shoulder and reached around to cup her breasts from behind. She hissed, arching her back and thrusting her breasts into his palms.

"Sex will help. Focus on your desire, your lust. It helps to lessen the need."

Andre plucked at her nipples and she moaned. It did help. Her mind focused on the pleasure as opposed to the mounting hunger. Her need shifted to her pussy, making her squirm.

"Will it always be like this?" she whined against Julian's lips as he leaned closer.

"No. It will get easier, and you will be able to control it."

He brushed his lips over hers and she sighed, pushing her hips back into Andre's engorged cock. He groaned and pinched her nipples harder, making her gasp as he rolled them between his thumbs and forefingers.

Tears gathered in her eyes and she squeezed her eyes tight. They escaped, flowing freely down her cheeks. Julian brushed them away with the pads of his thumbs. His lips soon followed, kissing away the tears so softly, she felt breathless.

He was so tender, so gentle, so understanding. Nothing like what she expected a full-blooded vampire to be. She knew of their beauty, their raw sexual appeal. She knew they could seduce. Even her mother had fallen prey to one…and then borne his child.

Her magical powers couldn't save her now. She had to rely on these two men. A vampire and a shape-shifter. Two men physically opposite, but both so unbelievably seductive and patient, she could hardly contain the lust raging through her body.

Julian nibbled at her lower lip, and her hands reached up to grip his upper arms. Her fingers dug into the hard muscle, leaving half-moons in his skin before sliding down his arms to leave red scratch marks on his flesh.

"Julian," she hissed as Andre moved one hand between her legs from behind and thrust two fingers deep into her aching pussy, fucking her with a slow rhythm.

With every thrust of his fingers, her hunger for the taste of blood grew along with the hunger for sex. She felt her fangs descend into place and she ran her tongue over the tips, drawing blood. Julian chose that moment to deepen the kiss. He sucked at her tongue and hot tingles ran down her spine, making her shudder.

Warm water sloshed around them, moved with them as they sandwiched her between their hard bodies. Oddly, she didn't feel trapped. She felt alive. Two husky males smothering her with attention sent her senses reeling and her hunger quickly climbing out of control.

"Hmmm, sweet," Julian murmured against her lips. "Do you think you can do this, Addison? Feed from Andre?"

She gasped, staring wide-eyed up at his questioning stare. She shook her head. "No. No. I'm not ready."

Unfortunately, just thinking about it made her mouth water. How could this be happening to her?

"You have to, angel."

The endearment caught her off guard and she blinked, unable to stop gazing into his beautiful blue eyes. She liked it. It felt right and for a moment made her forget what he'd been talking about.

"Turn around," Julian said, nodding behind her to Andre.

She turned to face Andre and swallowed. His gaze practically glowed with hunger as he watched her, and she swayed slightly. Andre' gripped her hands and pulled her along as he moved backward to the stone steps at the shallow end of the pool. He sat on the top step, tugging her until she stood between his legs.

His long cock stood past his navel. Soft white hair circled the base, and she fought the desire to run her fingers through it. That same white hair also covered his thighs and chest, almost invisible against his tan skin.

"You won't hurt me, Addy," he replied, trying to encourage her, but doubts plagued her despite the hunger stabbing her stomach.

Her hands began to shake uncontrollably and she gripped his fingers in desperation. She didn't want to do this. She couldn't do this but, at the same time, knew she couldn't not do it. It hurt too much. She had to stop the hunger before she lost her mind.

"It won't always be like this, Addy," Andre whispered as he pulled her to him.

He placed a soft kiss against her lips and she whimpered, sucking slightly at her fangs.

"Once you fully turn it will be much easier."

Addison shook her head, unsure she believed him. Julian moved behind her, placing his hands on either side of her hips. He leaned forward and bit softly at her shoulder and every inch of her flesh felt as though it were on fire.

"I want you to suck his cock, Addison," Julian commanded.

What happened to *angel*, and what did he want her to do? If she put that thing in her mouth, she would bite it. She knew she would. And once she tasted his blood, would she be able to stop?

"I'll help you, angel," Julian whispered. "I won't let you hurt him."

"Promise?"

She licked her lips, anxious to get him in her mouth for more than one reason. It wasn't just the blood; she was turned on. So damn turned on she could scream.

"It's okay, Addy," Andre whispered.

Reaching up, he cupped the back of her neck and drew her down to his engorged cock. He spread his legs and leaned back on his elbows as she gripped his base. He felt hot in her hands, like warm silk over hardened steel. Her heart raced in her chest to the point she thought it would burst. She bared her teeth, hissing slightly as his musky scent invaded her nose and the sound of his pulse overrode her own.

Just as she was about to engulf him in her mouth, Julian gripped a handful of her hair and held her back. Surprised, she gasped, then hissed softly.

"Easy," Julian growled, but not harshly. His voice was more husky from passion than anger. "Let me get it started for you. You might go too deep with your fangs."

Addison frowned. What? Was Julian going to bite into Andre's cock?

She watched in growing fascination as Julian leaned forward and slid his open mouth over Andre's cock. Andre moaned, his head dropping back, his eyes closing in pleasure. She'd never seen a man do this and part of her wanted to turn away, but she couldn't.

Julian sucked gently, his cheeks sinking in as he worked his mouth up and down the thick cock. Acting on instinct, she reached out and brushed Julian's hair from his face, getting a perfect, unobstructed view. Andre hissed as Julian's fangs scraped along the rod. Streams of blood escaped Julian's mouth and slid down to pool at Andre's balls.

Her heart pounded wildly. She needed to taste it.

Her fingers tensed in Julian's hair and he lifted his gaze to look at her. Releasing Andre's cock, he put his hand at the base of her neck and tugged her toward him.

"Lick his cock, angel. Slowly."

Hesitantly, she drew her tongue along the length of Andre's cock, lapping up the blood seeping from the shallow scrape. She shivered as the taste washed through her, warming her, filling her. She moaned and drew her tongue along his length again, starting at the base and working her way all the way to the tip before moving to his balls to lick the blood that had pooled there.

Andre gripped her hair, and at first she thought she might be hurting him, but when she looked at his face, all she saw was pleasure. Julian joined her, leaning down to lick the other side of his cock. At the tip, their lips met and he thrust his tongue inside, hungrily kissing her, his mouth mating wildly with hers.

My God, this is insane. She could come from the taste alone, from the heady feeling that gripped her as his blood mingled with hers. Seeing Julian do the same thing only made her desire rise. The flow of blood was beginning to ebb and she groaned, shoving Julian out of the way so she could engulf Andre's cock into her mouth. Sucking at it, she forced the flow back out again.

He groaned, lifting his hips, forcing his cock farther down the back of her throat. Her cheeks began to ache from stretching around his thick girth, but she couldn't stop. Her body moved of its own accord. The need drove her.

Lifting her hand, she gripped the base of his shaft and squeezed before dipping to his balls to massage them. They were high and tight, his hips lifting and thrusting. He was close. She could feel it. She could feel his rising lust, his tensing body, his racing heart. It washed through her like a tidal wave as he jerked upward, shouting as his cum filled her mouth. It mingled with the taste of blood, giving him a whole new flavor, and she savored the taste, knowing instinctively she would come to crave it.

"That's enough, angel."

She heard Julian's voice as though he were far away, knew she needed to stop, but couldn't. She heard Andre moan and felt his hand try to push her away, but despite that, she couldn't move from where she was.

Chapter Six

"Addison," Julian said much more firmly and punctuated his words with a tug on her hair. "Let him go."

With Julian's help, she managed to release his cock. Her harsh breaths filled the night around them, the need for her own release almost strangling her.

Julian leaned forward and slid his tongue gently along Andre's cock, stopping the slow flow of blood before standing to face her with a look that made her whole body flare in lustful hunger.

With a growl, she jumped forward, grabbing him around the neck and lifting her legs to circle his waist. His mouth slanted down on hers just as his hands gripped her hips, holding her steady as his huge cock found her entrance and thrust into her. She groaned, her hips working over him, her pussy sucking him deeper. His thickness stretched her, filled her, and she moaned, almost crying for him to fuck her harder. She needed him so badly, she could hardly breathe.

"God," she groaned against his mouth. "Oh, God."

Walking to the stairs, Julian climbed to the bottom one, then laid her on her back against the cold concrete next to Andre. His hands braced on the ground next to her shoulders as he pulled out slightly, then thrust back in so hard he took her breath away.

She gulped in air, her body struggling to accommodate him, struggling to accept his full length. He did it again, this time going deeper, giving her all of him. She moaned, her hips lifting to meet his thrusts, her legs circling around his hips to hold him to her.

Andre moved next to her, rolling over to gently suckle her breasts while Julian fucked her pussy.

"Oh, yes," she hissed as Andre's teeth nipped at her hard nipples.

Julian's thrusts increased, pistoning into her harder, deeper. The walls of her pussy clenched around him as she cried out for more. Her release was so close, her body craving it so badly.

Her fingers fisted and opened in Andre's hair, her nails scraping against his scalp. He murmured his approval and she opened her eyes to stare up at Julian. He looked amazing, his eyes glowing, his arms and stomach tensed as he moved in and out of her.

The sight, the sensations, was so amazing, so wild. The first stirrings of her climax raced along her flesh as Andre moved his hand from where it hung off the edge of the pool to her ass. Sliding his fingers to the tight hole of her anus, he spread the cream that had leaked from her pussy around the tiny opening. She moaned, panting now as Andre slid two fingers deep into her ass. Julian moaned as well, thrusting harder, faster.

"Like that, angel?" he murmured. "Do you like my fucking you with Andre's fingers in your ass?"

She whimpered, closing her eyes against the rising tide of sensations screaming through her. Not only her own, but theirs as well. It was too much. She needed it to stop.

"Julian," she sighed, shaking her head from side to side. "Oh, God. Make it stop. Make me come."

Andre matched Julian's rhythm, driving her insane. She never imagined this would feel like this. She was so full, so consumed, so damn overwhelmed. Her climax built, racing through her, choking her with its intensity.

She screamed as it took over. Julian fucked her so hard she thought she would scoot along the concrete, but she didn't care. Andre fucked her with his fingers while his lips placed gentle kisses along her ribs and stomach. So soothing. Julian tensed above her, shouting as his own release slammed through him. Turning his face toward the sky, he bared his fangs as his cum filled her pussy, his cock pulsing inside her.

Julian struggled with the desire to bite Addison. Not from the need to feed, but the need to make her his own. There was a difference, and it was that difference that rocked him to his soul. He needed to think, to put some distance between them. She was Sebastian's daughter, for crying out loud.

With a sigh, he touched the back of Andre's head. He'd laid his forehead against Addison's stomach, obviously weak from earlier. "Go to bed, Andre. You need to rest."

"We all do," he murmured.

"Yes…we do."

He glanced down at Addison's shocked face. He could feel her mortification, her shame, and part of him wanted to comfort her, but truthfully, he didn't know how. Not anymore. With a pang of regret, he pulled from her warm body and immediately felt the loss.

"It will be sunrise soon. We need to get back to the house."

Addison nodded but said nothing. Andre pulled his fingers from her body, then rose up to place a soft kiss against her forehead. She still had that deer-caught-in-the-headlights look, and he couldn't help but feel sorry for her. It would be crazy for a while. Nights filled with hunger, shifting emotions, and uncontrollable lust, both for blood and sex.

"Come on, Addison," he said, holding his hand out to her. "We'll need to help Andre."

Her worried gaze shifted to his friend, then back to him before she hesitantly placed her hand in his. He pulled her up, resisting the urge to kiss her again, to taste that sweet taste that was all her own.

Once on her feet, she glanced down at herself, her cheeks reddening adorably. She waved her hand and a robe appeared, covering her curves and filling him with disappointment. He enjoyed looking at her…way too much.

She caught him frowning and her own brow creased. "I forgot you don't like magic."

He shrugged. "It's fine, ang—Addison."

She appeared uncomfortable enough. Adding endearments would only make it worse, he was sure. Or at least he thought it would. He didn't miss the disappointment in her gaze before she turned away. Did she like angel?

He wasn't sure why he'd even started calling her that. He hadn't used pet names with a woman since Kayla. He'd called his former love baby, but Addison reminded him of a sweet angel, all soft and innocent…vulnerable.

"Would the two of you stop looking at each other all moony-eyed and help me the hell up?" Andre grumbled.

Julian snorted and stared down at his friend sprawled out on the concrete. The cuts on his cock were already healed, no visible sign left at all, just like always.

"I wasn't… I mean…" Addison stumbled and Andre smiled without opening his eyes.

"Yes you were, darlin'. You can't hide that kind of thing from me."

With a huff, she crossed her arms over her chest. "Just shut up, Andre."

"Ignore him," Julian said with a chuckle, enjoying her discomfort. "He gets off on making people squirm."

"I noticed," she grumbled, then kicked at Andre gently with her foot. "I didn't hurt you, did I?"

One corner of his mouth lifted in a small smile as he gazed up at her. A slight pang of jealousy gripped Julian at the interest clearly in his friend's gaze.

"Do I look like I'm hurt?" Andre asked, wiggling his eyebrows.

Addison studied him for a moment, her head tilted to the side. "Actually, you look quite satisfied."

"I am quite satisfied. You have a hell of a mouth on you, Addy."

Her face reddened and she glanced away, obviously uncomfortable.

"All right, shut up," Julian growled before leaning down to help his friend stand.

"Oh, I'm sorry," Andre purred. "Did you want a compliment on your mouth as well? I would never leave you out on purpose."

Julian's mouth thinned into a tight line. "Keep it up, smart-ass, and you'll walk back on your own."

With a grin, Andre cupped his cheeks and placed a quick kiss on his lips, making Julian chuckle. This kind of stuff was not unusual for Andre. They'd kissed before while seducing women. Women seemed to enjoy it, at least in their experience.

His gaze met Addison's surprised stare over Andre's shoulder, and he winked. Did she like seeing the two of them do this sort of thing? Would she like to see them do even more, or would it freak her out? That was something they would have to explore later.

"Come on, Addison. Let's get this ass back to the castle."

* * *

"This is your room," Julian said as he opened the massive wooden door.

Addison followed him into a large bedroom. A four-poster bed sat against a far wall facing a fireplace. Feeling chilly, she strolled over to the huge marble fireplace and waved her hand. A fire immediately blazed, flooding her with warmth.

Standing in this room was like being in another time. Period pieces filled the room, reminding her of an English manor or French castle. A beautiful blue and gold comforter covered the bed, and she ran her hand along the soft material, trying her best to forget that Julian watched her.

"It's beautiful," she sighed.

Her gaze lifted just a little, studying Julian through her lashes. He was still naked and didn't seem to be the least bit concerned by it. She, on the other hand, was completely mortified by her earlier behavior. Had she really allowed Andre to stick his fingers in her ass? And enjoyed it? And the blood. She could still feel the euphoria, the warmth that had spilled through her body as she'd fed from Andre. She shuddered, wiping at her lips, then studying her fingers, making sure no blood remained.

Julian strolled confidently across the room, his cock hanging enticingly between thick thighs, and she couldn't stop herself from watching him. Her gaze traveled upward past his washboard abs, hard pecs, and straight into an amused pair of heavenly blue eyes.

"You really should dress," she grumbled.

"Why? I'm going to bed."

Her eyes widened. "In here?"

He smiled slightly before turning and grabbing the corners of the thick velvet drapes. With one tug, he pulled them closed. "The sun is coming up. The drapes will keep the light out."

Interesting how he hadn't answered her. She licked her lips, trying to cover her embarrassment at blurting out that question. Why would he sleep here with her? Granted, the sex had been amazing, but they were just trying to help her through a rough night. The first of many, she was sure.

"Do you miss it?" she asked, trying not to look at his nude body.

"Miss what?"

"The sun."

Peeking at him, she caught a hint of sadness in his eyes before he turned away to head for the door. "I did at first."

"But now?"

He stopped at the foot of the bed and ran his palm over the intricate designs along the column. "I'm not sure I can even remember what daylight looks like."

His hand stopped about shoulder high and he turned his gaze to hers. They stood there, just staring at one another. She couldn't even begin to imagine how hard this life must have been for him. She knew how hard it was going to be for her. How much she would miss the sun and its warmth.

A single tear slipped down her cheek, and Julian stepped forward to wipe it away with the pad of his thumb. His touch was so gentle, his eyes so kind and understanding, she wanted to drown in them, to fall forward and let him enfold her in his arms and never let go.

"You'll get used to the darkness, angel," he whispered. "It takes time, but eventually you'll forget and accept."

He turned to leave the room, then shut the door behind him. Her lips trembled and her body shook in silent sobs as the truth of her destiny finally caught up with her. She would be a full vampire. Just like Julian. Just like her father.

Sitting on the edge of the bed, she allowed herself a few moments to wallow in self-pity, to allow herself to feel the despair of what she would now have to leave behind. Suddenly, she felt more alone than she'd ever felt in her life.

* * *

Julian strolled through the streets of Paris. The cool predawn air blew through his hair, and the smell of pastries and coffee filled his nostrils. He couldn't taste food anymore, but he could certainly smell it and sometimes he wished he couldn't. It was only a reminder of what he could no longer have.

He'd left the house right after depositing Addison in her room. Andre rested in the one next to her. Leaving might not have been the smartest thing to do, but he had to get out of the house for a while. What he'd taken from Andre had not been nearly enough. He needed to feed.

Something in the air around him made his skin prickle. His body tensed. He knew this feeling. Someone watched him.

His pace slowed as he took in the faces passing him on the street. Whoever they were, they were close. Too close. He would need to take care of them before he headed back to the castle. He couldn't afford for someone to follow him back.

As he walked, he tried to think of a way to flush them out.

An alley off to the right caught his attention and he slipped down it, hoping the others would follow. This older part of France reminded him of when he first turned. It was here in this ancient city, somewhere along these very streets. He'd made a rash decision…one that had cost him his very soul.

He moved into the shadows, fading into the darkness. He didn't have to wait long. Three men turned down the alley. Julian continued to remain still, watching. He wanted to make sure this was all of them. They knew he was here. They would be able to sense him just as he'd sensed them.

"I know he came down here," one of them murmured in French.

"He's here," the other replied, his accent more American.

"So Vlad sent the three of you to do his dirty work, I see," Julian replied as he stepped from the shadows, careful to keep all three vamps in front of him. "Too afraid to do it himself?"

The American smiled slightly. "I know of your reputation."

"And still you're here. You're either brave…or stupid." Julian took a step forward and two of the other vamps stepped back in reflex. An amused smile tugged at his lips.

The American hissed, baring his fangs. Julian snorted, ignoring the threat.

"Where's the woman?" the French vamp asked.

"What woman?"

"You know what woman," the American snarled. "We need her, Julian."

"What you need is your head examined," Julian snapped.

The other two vampires hissed, baring their fangs. Julian's eyes narrowed. He was much older than they and therefore more in control of his actions. Vlad should have known better than to send these whelps. He could take care of them with one hand and Vlad knew it. They had to be a distraction.

His heart jerked in his chest. Addison was in trouble.

"I don't have time for the three of you," Julian snarled.

"You'll make time," the American said as he stepped in front of Julian, blocking his path.

Julian growled low in his throat. His anger built, coursing through his body, and with it the hunger grew. Normally he didn't feed off vampires, but in this case, he would be willing to make an exception.

Lunging forward, he grabbed the American by the front of the throat, digging his nails deep into his flesh. The young man squirmed, his fingers trying to pry loose Julian's grip. Warm blood trickled down Julian's arm. The scent invaded his nostrils. Julian's fangs descended farther as he prepared to feed.

One of the others rushed forward to help, and Julian reached out with his free hand, grabbing him by the throat as well. He pulled him forward, sinking his fangs into the pulse at the side of his throat.

Warm blood pulsed into his mouth and he drank his fill until his victim became still. With vampires, the sweet taste would never come. They were already dead.

Julian let his victim's body fall limp to the ground at his feet. The American had become still, staring at him wide-eyed, his breathing harsh and erratic as Julian turned to face him.

The third man was off to his right, leaning against the wall, his face white as a sheet. It was obvious to Julian now just why these men were sent here. They weren't killers. They were idiots…stupid, scared young men who didn't know any better.

"Where's Vlad?" Julian snarled.

"We don't know," the American squeaked. "We were told to distract you."

Out of the corner of his eye he noticed a quick movement of the third man and Julian turned just in time to dodge a bullet as it whisked by his shoulder. As it did, he caught a whiff of silver and turned an angry glare on the young man who'd fired.

Silver would render him immobile. It was like a poison and, once in the bloodstream, would leave him paralyzed.

"I hope you have more than one," Julian snarled as he moved closer to him, the American still dangling from Julian's grip on his neck.

The young man's hand shook as he tried to aim the gun again. From out of nowhere, the gun ripped free from his hands and flew across the alley. Julian's son Marcus caught it with ease.

"*Jordush*," Marcus murmured, and the young man standing next to the wall morphed into a small roach.

With a snort, Julian quickly stepped on him, smashing him as he ground his foot and the bug into the concrete.

"Oooh," Marcus replied. "Harsh."

"Easier to explain a dead bug than a dead body." He turned to face his son. "What the hell are you doing here?"

Marcus nodded toward the end of the alley and the young woman watching them.

"Rebecca," Julian said in surprise.

She pointed to her chin, then nodded at him. Julian instantly knew what she meant and reached up to wipe his chin, removing the blood that had begun to dry.

"One of you needs to get to Addison," Julian said.

Marcus nodded to the man Julian still held. "We'll take care of him. You go to Addison."

Julian handed over the squirming American.

Rebecca stepped forward, her black shoes making soft clicks on the concrete. "The protection spell has not been breached, Julian. Addison is fine. If Vlad knows where she is, he hasn't figured out how to get to her yet."

"Yet." Julian turned to his son. "Meet me later. They were sent as a distraction. If our hiding place has been compromised, we'll need another."

"I agree."

With a wave of his hand, Julian disappeared in a puff of smoke, then reappeared at the castle. It was still daylight there and he stayed within the shadows as he traversed the castle halls, moving quickly toward Addison's room. He sensed nothing. No intruders, no hidden vampires. He wasn't sure what the distraction had been for. Had they found her and just not been able to breach the spell?

With a sigh, he stopped outside her door and pushed gently, hoping the door didn't squeak as it opened and wake Addison. Judging by the light, he had about four more hours to get sleep, and he would feel better if he could get it by her side.

He doubted she would like him sleeping with her, but he needed to be close. He didn't know why, didn't understand it. This feeling of protectiveness went far beyond just general protection.

With silent footsteps, he made his way to the bed. He studied her still, sleeping form. Her skin looked like creamy cappuccino against the stark white sheets. Her auburn hair spread across the pillow, and he reached out to run his fingers through the softness of her curls. Her full lips were slightly parted as though expecting a kiss from her lover and he fought down the urge to give her that kiss…to taste her again.

He ran the backs of his fingers down her arm and watched as goose bumps dotted her flesh. The sheet covered her breasts. He ran his fingers over the part that was exposed, enjoying the feel of her soft as cashmere skin. He could hear her heart beat, feel it like his own, and he dropped his hand away as the intensity grew. The separation did nothing to lessen the feeling.

Removing his clothes, he decided to wait until sunset to examine his feelings. Right now, he needed sleep. And he would sleep here, whether she liked it or not.

* * *

"I'm sorry. I can't break it."

Vlad growled, sending the young wizard flying across the room to land against the wall with a *thud.*

"You told me you could," Vlad snarled, baring his teeth to the cowering young man.

"I thought...I thought I could," he cried. "It's very powerful."

Vlad snarled, making the man cower and shake, bringing his hand up as though to ward off a blow.

"It's not going to work," Sorel said from the other side of the room. "Beating him to a pulp won't help your cause."

"It will help make me feel better," Vlad snapped toward him.

Sorel shrugged one shoulder. Deep brown eyes shone with indifference, and Vlad knew instinctively that deep inside that wizard beat the heart of the darkest evil.

"So what do you suggest?" Vlad asked.

"Let me handle it."

"You couldn't break the spell either."

"I'm not talking about using witchcraft. I'm talking about using our heads. I'll get on the inside."

"And how do you plan on doing that?"

"Trust me," he replied.

Chapter Seven

The heat from a warm body as it curled around hers seeped into her flesh, arousing her drowsy mind. A large, equally warm hand pressed gently against her stomach, just below her belly button, pulling her more tightly against him. Hard chest muscles pressed against her back and the coarse hair on his legs tickled the backs of hers. Even the length of his cock twitched ever-so-slightly against her hip. Just by the feel of his size alone, she knew it was Julian who lay next to her, his hard, massive body surrounding hers like a blanket.

Her stomach fluttered as her mind registered the fact he wore nothing. Not even a breath of air could slide between her and Julian. Sweat began to dot her brow and the places where Julian's skin touched hers. Was Andre here as well?

She darted her gaze around the room and saw nothing but the reddish gold designs the setting sun cast along the floor through the slit in the drapes. Taking a deep breath, she tried to calm her suddenly racing heart. She was alone with Julian. A man who had, just a few hours ago, fucked her senseless. And she'd let him, begged for it even.

The heat of a blush rushed over her cheeks. Surely there was a way to slip out of the bed without him knowing.

As slowly as possible, she moved his palm to her thigh. Instantly, his body stiffened and she froze, holding her breath.

"Going somewhere, Addison?"

His voice was soft and deep, almost like a caress in the darkened room. Goose bumps rose along her flesh as though he'd actually touched her, and she swallowed down a lump of rising desire.

"I thought you were still sleeping," she croaked, then cleared her throat softly.

"How are you feeling?" he asked.

She still couldn't turn and look at him. She swallowed again and then answered. "I've been better. Why are you in my bed?" Her lips thinned. "Naked."

"I sleep naked. As for the why…I thought it best you not be alone."

Her heart skipped. "Why? Did something happen?"

His chest expanded, then deflated as he let out a long sigh. Sitting up, she gripped the sheet to her chest and turned to face him. Her fingers shook slightly, tightening around the silk bunched just above her breasts. Julian rolled to his back, watching her through half-lowered lids. The sheet dropped to his waist and her gaze wandered aimlessly over his chest and stomach as her mind frantically tried to remember what they were discussing.

God, looking at him had been such a bad idea.

"Nothing that you need to worry about," he murmured.

Her eyes narrowed as she scrambled to focus on her anger and not the growing desire tightening her chest.

"Don't give me that look," Julian said, his lips twitching in amusement. The slight uplift to his mouth gave him an adorably roguish look that had her palms sweating.

"I'll give you more than a harsh look if you keep lying to me. What happened?"

Julian dragged the backs of his fingers down the sensitive flesh of her arm, and she jerked away, slapping at his hand. "Stop that."

After last night, she didn't think she was quite ready for round two. As good as it had been, he was still a stranger. And sex with strangers had never been her thing. But why couldn't she stop thinking about it? Wanting it? Moisture gathered in her pussy and she inwardly groaned. Why couldn't she stop needing it?

"Julian, please," she whispered as a tired sigh escaped past her lips.

His eyes rolled toward the ceiling as his hand dropped back to his chest. The other moved behind his head, supporting his neck. "I had a run-in with some of Vlad's men last night."

She drew in a sharp breath as the cold grip of fear wrapped itself around her heart. "Here?"

"No. France."

"What the hell were you doing in France?" she snapped.

His gaze shot back to hers. Mischief practically oozed from him and it surprised her. It was a side she hadn't expected and it threw her off guard.

"Worried about me?"

"Oh, give me a break." Snatching the sheet, she stood, purposely keeping her gaze off his cock, which now, thanks to her hasty retreat, lay in full view. With a growl of anger, she stomped over to the window and drew back the curtain, allowing the light from the full moon to spill across the floor. "It's my life that's in danger here. I think I deserve to be kept in the loop."

"Let's not forget that mine and Andre's lives are in danger, also, just by protecting you."

She started to open her mouth and say something, but Julian interrupted.

"Be quiet."

She gaped at him. "Excuse me?"

"I'm in charge of your protection, and if I feel it's better if you don't know, then you don't know."

"Why, you arrogant…"

He raised an eyebrow and she clamped her mouth tightly closed, silently fuming.

"Jerk!" she snapped after thinking it over. "You're not going to keep me in the dark, Julian. I forbid it," she snarled, moving closer to the bed. Her anger grew with every step.

"You forbid it?" he repeated, obviously amused, and she fought down the strangling desire to pick up something and throw it at him.

"Damn right I do. I'm not useless, you know. There are lots of things I can do to protect myself and you."

"With magic?"

"Yes. Magic."

Determined to prove her point, she twirled her finger and watched as his hands moved above his head. Leather straps circled his wrists, holding them in place against the headboard and keeping him trapped on his back. The amused expression on Julian's face turned to outright surprise, then fury. She shivered but quickly recovered, sending him a sweet smile.

"See?"

"Undo me, Addison," he growled. "Now."

"I think not."

"I think you'd better…or suffer the consequences when I get free."

And just what might those be?

"I'm not a child, Julian."

"Then stop acting like one and let me out of this."

His hands jerked at the leather, but it held, and she breathed a silent sigh of relief. Despite the stirring of lust his threat of consequences raised, she wasn't quite ready to let him free yet.

"Not until we get something straight."

Andre's laughter filled the room and she turned in surprise toward the door, where he stood practically doubled over, his whole body shaking. "Well, well," he said with a chuckle as he straightened to lean against the doorjamb. With one hand, he wiped at the moisture gathering in his eyes. "Never thought I'd see this."

"Shut the hell up, Andre, and get these straps off me."

"I don't know," Andre drawled, obviously enjoying himself. "I think I like you as the submissive. What brought this on, anyway?"

"He won't tell me what happened last night."

"We fucked by the pool," Andre replied, and her face heated in embarrassment.

"Not *that*. I remember that," she snapped. "After that. In France."

Andre stood straight and pushed away from the doorjamb. His face scrunched in worry as he moved to stand over Julian. "What the hell were you doing in France?"

"Feeding," Julian snarled. "Which I'm about to do again, if you don't get me out of this."

Andre's brow rose. "You think threatening to feed off me is scary?" Andre snorted, then turned to face Addison. "I don't think letting him go now would be a very good idea. He's livid."

Addison shrugged. "I have no intentions of letting him go, anyway. He hasn't told me anything yet."

"Damn the both of you to hell," Julian grumbled.

"What the hell is going on in here?"

Both Addison and Andre turned to look at Marcus, who stood just inside the doorway, his lips tightening, fighting a grin. Another woman Addison didn't recognize came into the room as well, then stopped dead in her tracks. Her eyes widened in surprise before she burst into bright laughter.

"For the love of God," Julian murmured from his spot on the bed.

"Am I interrupting something?" Marcus asked, his voice dripping with obvious amusement.

"Nothing other than my humiliation," Julian snapped.

"Your father is a stubborn jackass," Addison replied as she attempted to adjust the sheet she still held closed at her chest.

Marcus chuckled as the woman covered her mouth with her hand and cleared her throat with a dainty cough.

"Didn't take her long to figure *you* out, I see." Grabbing a blanket off the chair by the fireplace, Marcus threw it over his father's waist, covering him. Julian rolled his eyes but remained silent.

"Silence is a sure sign my father is pissed," Marcus said with a grin.

Addison studied him, wondering at the smile. Did everyone but her find this funny? "*You* don't seem very concerned."

"It's not me he's pissed at."

She slapped at her thigh with her palm in aggravation. "I just want to know what happened last night in France. Have they found me already?"

"Yes." The woman from the doorway spoke.

"Who are you?" Addison asked.

"I'm Rebecca. I'm a friend of Marcus and Julian's."

"She's also a member of the witch's council," Andre said. "She's the one who put the protection spell in place around the castle."

"The spell hasn't been breached, but they know she's here. The spell has weakened from the attack against it. I'm afraid even black magic will not keep them out for long. Not since they know she's here."

Anxiety knotted Addison's stomach, and she tightened her fingers around the edges of the sheet to stop their trembling. How had they found her so fast?

"If they could find me here, where else could I possibly hide?"

"I know of a place." Julian sighed from his spot on the bed.

"Can I release him?" Rebecca asked, and Addison nodded, although a bit reluctantly.

With a wave of her hand, Rebecca freed Julian's wrists from the bindings. His hands dropped to the bed and he quickly sat up, rubbing at his wrists. His piercing gaze held Addison immobile as he stood and walked over to stand directly in front of her. He appeared completely comfortable in all his naked glory and she couldn't stop staring at him, at his confidence, his raw, masculine sex appeal.

"You will pay for that," he growled quietly, and Addison raised her chin in defiance, despite the erotic tingles skimming under her skin.

"Jeez, Julian," Marcus sighed.

With a wave of Marcus's hand, clothes appeared on Julian, whose eyes narrowed dangerously toward his son. "I can dress myself."

"It was taking you too long," Marcus snapped back, hands on hips.

With that expression and stance, he looked just like his father. Apparently, Addison wasn't the only one to notice. Andre did as well and chuckled before replying, "There's no denying he's your child, is there?"

Addison sighed, rolling her eyes toward the ceiling. "Can we move back to the subject of my protection, please? Where do we go from here?"

"We leave here for two hours, let Rebecca dismantle the spell, then create one somewhere else. Once that spell is in place, we return here," Julian replied, and Addison gaped at him.

"Are you insane?"

"Actually," Marcus mused as he dropped onto the edge of the bed, "that's not a bad idea. They wouldn't expect you to stay here, and the spell will be a diversion of sorts."

Addison frowned as a pain began to form in her stomach. She winced, dropping one hand to cover her stomach. Hunger grew and she took deep breaths to try to control it. She didn't need this now. There was a room full of people needing to work out a new plan. A plan to protect her.

"Addison?" Julian asked softly, suddenly very close to her.

Too close. She could feel his heat, hear his heartbeat, smell his musky scent and the blood coursing through his veins.

"I don't feel very well," she whispered.

"How far along is she in the ascension?" Marcus asked.

"Further than she should be," Julian replied.

"It's always faster and harder on the ones who will be full-blooded."

Her gaze met Julian's as a single tear slipped free to fall down her cheek. Jumbled and quickly changing emotions left her feeling like a rag doll. The hunger left her feeling like a beast. In his eyes, she saw understanding, a kindred spirit. A soul mate.

"Andre, why don't you help Addison with a shower, while I talk with Marcus?" Julian suggested.

Andre came forward and gently cupped her elbow, pulling her away from Julian. "Come on, Addy. Let's let them work this out."

Addison nodded and followed behind Andre as though in a daze. Her limbs felt heavy, her mind muddled.

"Julian entranced me again, didn't he?" she asked as they made their way through the castle halls. The farther away from the room they went, the better and more in control she felt. Pain again sliced through her stomach and she winced.

"If he did, he probably thought it best you didn't argue."

"He can't keep doing that to me," she said, her aggravation growing. "Can't I stop him from doing it?"

"Julian has had eight hundred years to perfect that. It will take you time to figure out how to fight it."

"But I can fight it?" she asked.

Andre nodded his head slightly. "Possibly."

She frowned. "You're a lot of help."

A small smile tugged at his lips. "I'll help you with a lot of things, Addy, but I won't help you fight Julian right now. You need to do as he says, at least for a little while longer. If the three of us survive this, then I'll help you fight him all you want."

"What makes you think the three of us will still be together?"

"That's an easy one to answer, but I'll let you figure it out on your own."

With a huff of exasperation, she tugged at the sheet trailing the ground behind her and pulled it up slightly. This was going to be another rough night; she could feel it.

They stepped into a massive bathroom with beige-colored stone tiles and cherry cabinets. A huge tube sat before a large window overlooking the grounds. A stone archway made the tub appear as though it were nestled within a small cave. Beside it was a huge shower stall.

Andre tugged at her sheet and she jerked her head around to stare at him, her shaking hands holding the material to her like a lifeline.

"It's okay, Addy. It's not like I haven't seen you naked."

Andre was so sweet, so comforting. She felt safe with him. Completely opposite of how she felt when she stood close to Julian. Julian made her feel safe, but he also left her feeling somewhat out of control.

She nodded and let the sheet fall to the floor. Andre's gaze wandered lazily over her body, and her flesh heated. Every inch of her came alive at the look of desire shining in his eyes. Was this a true reaction to him, or her body's oversensitized emotions taking over? Julian said everything would be intensified over the next few days until her body became used to the heightened state of her senses.

"A shower will make you feel better," Andre whispered as he gently pushed her toward the stall.

Reaching in, he started the water and then stepped back to remove his own clothes. Addison watched, enthralled as every piece of material fell to the floor, exposing his lean, muscular physique. He was built so different from Julian, and so incredibly beautiful in his own way. Her gaze wandered over his runner's thighs, then upward over washboard abs. When she reached his face, his sparkling eyes and sexy grin made her breath catch.

Andre stepped into the shower and checked the water temperature before turning on the sprayers. Warm water hit her body from three sides, relaxing the tense muscles, but unfortunately not relieving the gnawing pain. Cramps tightened her stomach in ever-increasing intensity.

She sighed, letting the spray wash away her anxiety, trying to let it wash away the hunger.

"You're cute when you do that," Andre whispered as his hands gently cupped her cheeks, tilting her head so the water could wet her hair.

"Do what?" she asked, dropping her head back even more, letting the water wash over the top of her head and down the back of her neck.

"When you sigh it sounds as though you're in heaven."

She smiled slightly, enjoying the feel of his thumbs as they massaged along her hairline. "I feel like I'm in heaven right now. Between the heat of the water and the feel of your fingers, I could melt into a puddle."

Warm, soft lips touched her brow, and her breathing momentarily stopped.

"What does that do?" he whispered seductively, sending tingles of awareness to every inch of flesh.

"More than I expected," she admitted, and she felt his lips spread into a smile as they brushed against her temple.

Lower they traveled, along her cheek and jawline, making her stomach tighten in growing need. She inhaled a deep breath, drawing in his spicy scent. Mingled in it was the smell of his blood, and hunger gnawed at her insides with a force that tensed her whole body.

"I hate this feeling," she whimpered.

Licking her lips, she tried to fight the rising need.

"It will get better," Andre whispered against her ear.

His fingers kept massaging, moving down her neck in slow, tantalizing strokes that made her heart race wildly.

"In the meantime, you always have me to ease the ache."

She shook her head in denial, unsure she was mentally ready to feed again. It still disgusted her, despite the fact the very idea of doing it almost sent her body straight into orgasm. Just the memory of how his blood had tasted made her want it all the more.

"It's okay, Addy." Andre's lips brushed against the sensitive flesh below her ear, making her shudder. "I won't let you hurt me. I've done this enough with Julian to know what to expect and how to handle it. You need to do this. Just a little will quell the hunger and allow you to think more clearly, and Julian needs you clear right now."

Deep down she knew he was right. She did need a clear head. She needed to be able to help them, not be a hindrance because she fought her hunger.

Andre turned her so she faced the back tile wall. The spray of water hit her breasts, and her nipples hardened as the erotic sensation shot straight to her pussy.

Andre put his wrist before her lips and she hesitated, staring at the smooth bit of flesh. His pulse beat just below the skin. She could feel it in her own veins. Her fangs descended and she licked her tongue across the tips, sighing as the warm, spicy taste of her own blood filled her mouth.

Andre's other arm circled her shoulders, holding her close to him, and her head lowered toward his arm. He had so much faith in her, so much trust. If she were in his shoes, she would be terrified of what might happen. What if he couldn't control her like he thought?

"I trust you, Addy," Andre whispered, and she surged forward, grasping his arm with both hands and sinking her teeth into the soft flesh.

Andre hissed and dropped his face into her neck. Addison could hardly think straight as his blood spilled into her mouth with every beat of his pulse. As she sucked, her heart began to beat in time with his and euphoria consumed her. Her body warmed and strengthened, pulsing further to life with every sip of his blood.

As her hunger lessened, another form of lust began to take hold. Just like last night, her pussy clenched in need, desperate for the feel of his cock buried deep inside her.

Breaking her mouth away from his wrist, she watched as the blood spilled from his wrist onto the tile.

"Lick your tongue across it," Andre whispered. "It will close the wound."

For a split second, she hesitated, wondering if she could put her mouth to his wrist without sucking more blood. Taking a deep breath, she brought his wrist back to her lips and drew her tongue across the puncture holes. They closed instantly and she stared in fascination.

"You can only do that to a vampire bite. It will not work on any other wound."

She nodded, still trying to fight the lust humming through her veins. "Why do I feel so damn horny?" she growled, slowly losing the battle of mind and heart over body.

"That will also get better with time," Andre whispered as he placed soft butterfly kisses along her neck.

Her head tilted to the side, allowing him better access. Wetness pooled in her pussy, and she squeezed her legs together, trying to ease the growing need centered there.

"Do you want me to ease the ache, Addy?" Andre asked.

Without thinking twice, she nodded, almost desperate now for some relief.

Andre leaned her against the wall in the corner and she sagged, her body going limp against the cool, wet tiles. He dropped to his knees before her and gently placed one of her feet against the small seating ledge built into the wall.

Soft lips kissed the inside of her thigh and she gasped, tilting her pussy toward his face, seeking the touch she knew would send her over the edge.

She buried her hands in his hair and tried to tug him toward her, make him put his mouth where she wanted him to. Andre chuckled and softly blew against her clit. Her whole body trembled as a wave of pleasure shook her to the core.

My God. All he'd done was blow against it. Heaven help her if he was to fully touch the sensitive nub.

Every part of her tensed with anticipation as he used the tips of his fingers to separate her labia. His thumb brushed across her clit, smearing juices around the tiny hub of sensitivity.

She gasped, drawing in deep breaths of air to try to calm her raging lust. A sense of being watched came over her, and she opened her eyes, staring straight into Julian's. He stood in the doorway of the shower, naked, his cock long and hard, his eyes narrowed and glowing with desire.

Her heart practically jumped from her chest at the sight of him. All masculine male and hungry. She'd never had a man look at her the way he and Andre did. She'd never reacted to someone the way she reacted to them. It was all she could do at times to keep from attacking them, taking them both into her willing body.

"Julian," she sighed.

Her fingers gripped Andre's head harder, flexing in his hair as her desire consumed her.

Julian stepped into the shower. Water droplets clung to his shoulders and chest, glistening beneath the soft lights of the room.

"Did you feed?" he asked, and she nodded.

He placed his hand on Andre's head as he glanced down at him. "Are you okay?"

"Do I not look okay?" Andre asked snidely, making Julian grin.

"Resume what you were doing, Andre, and forget I asked." His piercing gaze met hers, and she could hardly breathe at the lust staring back at her. "I think I'll just watch for a minute."

Andre slid his tongue along her slit and she gasped. Moaning and undulating her hips against his face, she sought a more firm touch, anything to ease this burning hunger. Andre moaned his approval, licking his fill of her cream as it leaked from her pulsing channel.

"You're beautiful," Julian whispered.

When he looked at her like that, she felt beautiful. The thought that he watched her as Andre ate out her pussy didn't even enter her mind. It seemed natural, as though they'd been doing it forever.

"Absolutely beautiful," he whispered again as he reached up to pinch at her nipples. She moaned, closing her eyes as waves of pleasure soared through her veins.

"Like that?" he teased. "What about this?"

Using his palm, he cupped one breast and squeezed. She groaned, shifting between arching her back and thrusting her hips.

She was so close. She could feel it just beyond her reach and she wanted it so badly.

"Can you take us both, Addison?" Julian murmured against her mouth, and she opened her lips, silently begging for him to kiss her. "Me in your pussy and Andre in your ass?"

About that time, Andre thrust two fingers into her pussy and she screamed, dipping her knees to take him deeper.

"Or vice versa," Julian said with a grin. "Because I would love to feel that ass of yours as you come."

She whimpered, imagining in her mind what he was saying. It made her crazy, filled her with a burning need she didn't even know existed. Her anal muscles contracted and Andre groaned, increasing the thrust of his fingers, fucking her harder, deeper, faster. His tongue flicked across her clit, then flattened, teasing the tight little bud until she screamed.

Her vision blurred as wave after wave of pleasure screamed through her, robbing her of every sight and sound except for her two men.

"Oh…my…God," she sighed, sagging back against the wall as Andre continued to slowly stroke her pussy with his palm.

"Feeling better?" Julian asked as his lips brushed across her cheek. It was such a sweet caress of his mouth against her flesh. Andre kissed her stomach and then rested his forehead just below her belly button. Embarrassed, she realized she still held handfuls of his hair and quickly released him, relaxing her fingers.

"I'm not sure if I feel better or worse. How do you deal with this?" she asked, still slightly breathless.

"Once you fully turn, the lust for sex after you feed will diminish. Right now, your body is just trying to adjust. The euphoria you feel when you feed is much like an orgasm.

You haven't learned how to fully control it, so the lust runs rampant."

"So…" She licked her lips nervously, unsure she should really ask the one question she needed an answer to. "So the desire I feel for you and Andre isn't real but the euphoria from feeding?"

"That's for you to decide," Julian said as he leaned down to gently brush his lips across hers.

They were so soft, like butterfly wings, and she found herself wanting more. She wanted to taste him, feel his mouth against hers. He pulled away much too soon and she swallowed down the desire to call him back.

Instead, she tried to focus on her protection. Anything to get her mind off the sex and her hunger for blood, which continued to simmer within her gut.

"Where's Marcus and Rebecca?" she asked.

"I was about to ask the same thing," Andre replied.

Julian's lips lifted into a tiny smile as he touched the top of Andre's head with his palm. "They left to transfer the spell."

"Aren't we supposed to leave?" she asked.

"I changed my mind. I think we should stay here. Once Vlad realizes the spell is gone, he'll try to relocate it. Hopefully, thinking we went with it."

"Is that a good idea?" Andre asked.

"Time will tell. Her blood will be the most powerful on the night of her ascension. As it gets closer, Vlad will get more desperate."

"You guys can't hide me forever." She sighed tiredly. "And I don't want to run forever."

"You won't have to," Julian said as he brushed her wet hair from her brow. "But I want you more in control of things before we face them. And you will eventually have to face them."

A dark shadow passed over Julian's gaze, and a terrible feeling of foreboding washed over her.

* * *

"What or who were you before you became a vampire, Julian?"

Julian looked up from the fire to stare at Addison. What had she asked him? All he could seem to think about was how she'd looked earlier. Her face flushed, her eyes wild with passion, her body undulating. The whole scene had been so damn sexy, he couldn't get it out of his head.

He should have fucked her. He should have done it right then and gotten it out of his system. If he had, maybe he'd have been able to think more clearly over the last couple of hours.

She'd used magic to conjure up clothes, and right now, lounging on the couch in those jeans and sweater, he couldn't remember her ever looking more pretty or desirable.

Her brow rose in curiosity as she watched him and he swallowed, thinking quickly of something to say.

"You didn't hear what I asked, did you?" she said, amusement tilting her lips.

"No," he admitted reluctantly, then gave her a half smile. "I'm sorry. My mind was…elsewhere."

"I think that was rather obvious. Where was it?"

"On you, actually," he replied, watching her closely.

He hadn't felt this kind of emotional turmoil since Kayla, and it unsettled him, made him uncomfortable.

"Me? What about me?"

"Keeping you safe."

Her mouth formed a silent O as apprehension darkened her eyes. He hadn't meant to worry her. She'd looked like she was finally beginning to relax. "What did you ask me, Addison? I'll try to pay better attention this time."

She smiled slightly, the spark returning to her gaze if only for a moment. "How did you turn? Where you bitten?"

"Yes. A Frenchman by the name of Renee."

She shook her head. "Why? Did you ask for it?"

"No. I was at the wrong place at the wrong time."

"How so?"

"I walked in on him, sort of. He was feeding in an alley, not far from where I was staying in France. I tried to help his victim and, as a mortal, was quickly overwhelmed. He told me later my bravery intrigued him. When I think back on it, I think it was more stupidity than bravery."

Addison chuckled and Julian moved to sit next to her on the sofa.

"So he turned you that night instead of killing you?"

"Yes. Right there in that alley, a stupid human died and a vampire was born."

"Do you regret it?"

"It does no good to regret. I've learned to live with it."

"How long were you with him?"

"Over fifty years."

"What happened to him?"

Julian was silent as memories of that night ran through his mind. He hadn't thought about this in centuries. "He was murdered. I found him just before dawn impaled on a stick, his body charred."

"Oh my God," Addison whispered. "Did you know who did it?"

"Yes."

"Well?" she asked, indicating with a roll of her hand she wanted him to continue.

"Let's just say they met the same fate. I was a coldhearted bastard back then, Addison. I still am."

She shook her head. "I don't believe that."

He smiled slightly. "You don't have to believe it for it to be true."

"If you're so coldhearted, why are you helping me?"

"Because I believe vampires should stay in the shadows. I believe we can feed without taking lives. And I prefer not to be hunted, which is exactly what would happen if your father had his way. Vampires would rule and mortals would be nothing more than food. A war would break out. A war humans would lose." He shrugged. "I like things the way they are."

"My father is coldhearted, Julian. You're not."

She reached out and fingered his hair, rubbing the strands between her thumb and forefinger. A huge part of him wanted to reach out to her. To feel again. He'd been rejected once for what he was. Granted, she was turning. She would be just like him. That didn't mean she would accept him or the love he could offer her. She could die or, God forbid, choose to help her father. He couldn't live with the pain of losing someone again. He had to harden his heart, not fall under her spell. He had to keep things strictly physical and nothing more.

He quickly stood and her hand fell away. She remained silent, her expression thoughtful as she watched him. He felt the loss of her touch like a punch and missed the heat of her body as he moved to stand by the fire.

Say something, he thought to himself.

"You're awfully moody," she said, surprising him, and he jerked his head up to stare at her.

"What?"

"You're moody. I touched you and you jumped up like you'd been shot."

"That's not being moody."

"Yes it is. We were talking, learning things about each other, and then suddenly there's a wall there. A big one."

He blinked, unsure quite what to say. He'd tried to put some distance between them, and she'd called him on it.

"There's not a wall, Addison. I just…" *Just what? Just needed some space between you and me?*

Hell, what he really wanted to do was kiss her.

One corner of her lips lifted in an amused tilt. "I made you flustered."

He snorted. "I don't get flustered."

Her grin widened, but quickly as it had come, the smile faded and her gaze wandered to the window. "What do we do now?"

"As far as protection?"

"Yes," she replied, returning her gaze to his.

God, he could drown in those beautiful eyes. He could still see the desire from earlier simmering just below the surface, but mingled with that desire was also fear.

"The spells are gone, so that means Andre and I will have to take turns guarding you. Andre will take the day shift, and I'll take the night. At least until Marcus returns with help."

"Where is Andre?"

"He's taking a nap." Julian couldn't resist a grin. "It seems you wore him out earlier."

A blush moved over her cheeks and she glanced away, bringing her finger to her mouth to chew on her nail. It was the first time he'd seen her do that. It was very endearing and made him want to hold her, let her know it would all be fine.

He hoped.

"Maybe we should let them take me," she murmured.

Julian frowned. Surely he hadn't heard her correctly. "What?"

"You said earlier I'll have to face them eventually. Why put it off? The sooner it's done, the sooner I can get on with my life."

"You're not ready."

"Will I ever be ready?"

Julian licked his lips and sighed. "Addison. No one is ever ready to do what you are going to have to do. But right now, you have zero control. And you know it."

"What if they are able to get me? What exactly do they want to do to me?"

"From what we can gather, Sebastian is in a suspended, magical state. He's existing somewhere between life and death. He needs blood; unfortunately, only blood of a direct descendant or parent will work."

"It's obvious that I'm going to be a full vampire. So they won't need to kill me, correct?"

Julian hesitated, then decided it was best to tell her the truth. "We're not sure." Taking a deep breath, he continued. "Sebastian was badly burned. He'll need to rejuvenate his flesh as well as his soul. So that may require more of your blood."

"Does it have to be done on the night of my ascension?"

"That's when your blood will be at its most powerful for what they have in mind."

She nodded, but he could tell the wheels in her head were spinning about something. He suddenly became suspicious.

"What are you turning over in your mind, Addison?" he asked, narrowing his gaze on her.

She looked at him in surprise, then shook her head. "Nothing."

"Nothing at all?"

"No."

He didn't believe her for a second.

Chapter Eight

Addison stood back, leaning against the wall. With her hands clasped behind her back, she shifted slightly, pressing her butt against the cold stone. A few feet away, Julian and Andre were talking, their soft voices barely audible. She could make out words here and there, but nothing more. Not enough to tell her what they were talking about.

Both of them looked so handsome, she had to stop herself from sighing at just the sight of them. Andre held a sandwich in his hand, one foot on the raised hearth of the fireplace, his free hand grasping the mantle. He wore jeans and a T-shirt, his feet bare.

Julian stood close to him, his stance more refined. One hand in his pocket, the other on the mantle next to Andre's, their heads bent in close. Part of Julian's hair fell over his shoulder, obscuring a little of his face, and she imagined brushing it back. She knew it would be soft. She'd felt it earlier before he'd pulled away from her.

She knew he'd been hurt in the past. Was that why she had this feeling he didn't fully trust her? She could see it in his eyes sometimes. The suspicions. The questions.

Andre, on the other hand, didn't seem to have any problem with her. He openly flirted, touched her, and made her smile more often than not. Julian brooded, watched her; he made her nervous and, at the same time, made her want him. If she wasn't careful she'd end up falling for one or even both of them. Two men were never more completely opposite, and never more attractive.

But no doubt about it, she had to survive first.

She blinked, staring at Andre in slight confusion as the expectant look on his face shifted to concern.

"I'm sorry, did you say something?" she asked.

"I asked how you were feeling?" Andre replied.

"I don't know. Confused. Scared. Tired." She shrugged. "My father wants to drain my blood to bring himself back to life. How should I be feeling?"

Andre grinned. "Damn glad to be alive?"

"Ha-ha," she replied. "Maybe I should live my life as though these last few days are all I have?"

Andre's lips twitched slightly. "And what would you do?"

She pursed her lips, thinking. "Visit France. I've always wanted to." Then she frowned as a profound sadness gripped her, tightening her chest. "Or see the sunrise over the ocean one last time, feel the heat of the sun on my face."

She looked at Julian and felt like weeping at the longing in his eyes. She knew instinctively it was a longing for the things she'd mentioned. The life he missed just as much as she would. Briefly, she wondered if there was something she could do to help him. Maybe there was a spell she could cast that would allow him at least a few hours in the sun.

"I could take you to see the sunrise," Andre offered.

She blinked in surprise. She hadn't expected him to take her seriously.

"I'm not sure that's a good idea," Julian grumbled.

"Why?" Andre asked. "I would have Marcus go with us as added protection. Or what about Rebecca's husbands, Nicholas and Darien?"

"Nicholas and Darien are in Germany with the council. Tonya, Rebecca, and Marcus are at Rebecca's home, researching, I believe."

"You don't trust me alone with her?"

Julian growled softly. "It's not that, idiot. If you take her out during the day, I can't help you if you get into trouble."

Addison scowled angrily. "You know. If I remember correctly, I think I did a pretty good job of protecting myself that night in New Orleans. I believe I'm capable of doing it again."

"It's not a chance I'm willing to take. If you want to see the sunrise, you'll do it here."

"That's ridiculous. I can transport us to the Caribbean and right back again in seconds."

"No."

Despite his softly spoken command, the look in his eyes let Addison know there would be no argument. Even Andre remained quiet, but Addison didn't know when to quit.

"Are you always such a bossy, arrogant jerk? I haven't taken orders from someone in quite some time. I'm not about to start again now."

Julian's gaze narrowed, his blue eyes sparkling with anger. "You know damn good and well what's at stake,

Addison. Don't do anything foolish just because you don't like being told what to do."

She pushed away from the wall, hands on hips. "Maybe it's just your tone that pisses me off."

Julian turned to Andre. "Would you do something with her?"

"Excuse me?" Addison exclaimed.

"Me?" Andre asked, turning his finger to point at his own chest. "You started this, my friend. Don't be a coward; finish it."

"A coward?" Julian bellowed.

"You always take off at a full run whenever things with women start to get interesting. You don't want her to go to the ocean, convince her to stay here yourself."

With that, Andre walked to the other side of the room. Julian licked his lips, sighing as he glanced around the room, anywhere but at her. She was beginning to see he did that quite frequently when he was agitated. She crossed her arms over her chest, waiting.

Finally, after a couple of moments of silence, Julian spoke. "I don't think it would be a good idea to go to the ocean, Addison."

"Why?" she asked stubbornly.

His eyes met hers and suddenly she couldn't breathe. In his gaze, she could see everything she herself felt—desire, confusion, anxiety. It was almost like looking in a mirror.

"Because I don't want you to get hurt," he replied softly.

"Why?" she asked again, her heart pounding as she waited for his answer.

"I don't know," he whispered.

What?

"You don't know?"

"You're the daughter of one of my former lovers, Addison."

She swallowed, shocked at his admission. Okay, even she could admit that was a little odd.

She shrugged. "So?"

"Your father tried to kill my son. I don't know what will happen if he gets his hands on you. Will you go to him? Will you help him?"

"Why would I? I don't know him. Don't want to know him. I have no intentions of helping him, Julian. Is that really what concerns you? Or are you just afraid of having another woman turn away from you?"

Julian's gaze widened slightly in surprise.

"You know," Andre replied from the entrance to the room, a slight smile on his face as he leaned against the doorjamb. "She sure figured you out in a hurry."

Julian rolled his eyes and glanced back toward the fire. She doubted she would get a straight answer from him now.

* * *

Addison walked the perimeter of the basement lab, running the tips of her fingers over the bottles lining the shelves. There was so much here. Everything she could possibly need was at her fingertips.

Why hadn't anyone done this for him before? Everything needed for the spell was on the shelves.

She'd never done a spell like this, and part of her was quite apprehensive. What if it didn't work? He would burn before they could get him back inside. But she had to try.

The look of longing in his eyes at the mention of watching the sunrise tugged at her heart. She wanted him to see it. She wanted to share her last sunrise with Julian.

After grabbing one of the bottles, she quickly moved to the work space in the center of the room. A thick layer of dust covered the wooden table, but with a wave of her hand she removed it, leaving in its place a gleaming surface.

She pulled the book she'd found in the library closer to better see the list of ingredients listed on its pages. With a quick glance toward the door, she turned and grabbed one of the bowls off the shelf behind her and began mixing the final ingredients.

The spell's simplicity surprised her. A small drop would be enough, but it would have to be entered into his bloodstream for it to work. The spell would last longer on her than it would on him. He was much older, and the older the vampire, the shorter time the spell would last.

Taking a knife, she mixed the ingredients, creating a black, thick paste. Once the paste was the proper consistency, she scraped the paste out of the bowl and into a tiny crystal cup.

"That should do it," she murmured with a smile and headed out of the lab and back up the stone steps to the main level.

She came up through the back hall, almost running smack into Andre, who gave her an uncharacteristic scowl of impatience.

"Where the hell were you?" he snapped, shaking her shoulders. "God, Addison. You scared the hell out of us."

His tone startled her and she took a step back, staring at him in surprise and cradling the small cup in her palm. "I was in the lab."

"I found her," he yelled down the hall before turning to cup her cheeks in his hands. "I'm sorry I yelled, Addy. But you scared the hell out of me."

"You said that already," she said, her lips twitching slightly.

Out of the corner of her eye she saw Julian make his way down the darkened hall. He didn't stroll, he stomped, his gaze shining in fury, and her breath caught in her throat.

Andre was sweet, tender. Julian was… God, Julian was magnificent.

"Damn it, Addison," he snapped as he came closer. "Don't ever run off like that again, do you understand? You don't go anywhere unless you tell us first."

Andre dropped his hands from her face, and she took an unconscious step back. "Okay, I get it."

"Where the hell were you?"

"In the lab."

"Doing what?" he snapped.

She frowned, her own anger taking hold and robbing her of her better judgment. "After the way you're talking to me, why the hell should I tell you?"

"All right," Andre began, trying to intervene. "We found her, she's fine. Relax."

"Don't fucking tell me to relax!" Julian snarled.

Andre's hands moved to his hips, and his eyes narrowed in anger. "I put up with a lot of crap from you, Julian. Don't push it."

Addison watched them in surprise. This was a side of Andre she hadn't expected to see. He was actually standing up to Julian. Should she come between them?

Stepping forward, she decided the last thing she wanted was for them to get into a fight. She put her back to Andre and turned to face Julian and his fury head-on.

"I was down in the lab making something for you," she said.

Julian looked at her blankly for a second. "From magic?"

"Does it matter?"

"Yes," he said before turning to walk away.

"Fuck you then," she snapped and threw the cup.

He turned just in time to catch it in his hand. He stared at it, then glanced back at her. "What is this?"

"It was made with magic," she said as she strolled past him, refusing to acknowledge the hurt his rejection had caused her. "What do you care?"

She walked quickly down the hall, determined to not look behind her. Tears burned the backs of her eyes, and she wiped at them with shaking fingers. God, what was wrong with her? Why was she being such a baby?

Julian watched her go and felt like kicking himself in the ass. He looked back at Andre, who still stared at him angrily. "I know. I'm an ass," Julian grumbled.

"You said it," Andre replied, making Julian smile slightly.

Julian lifted the cup, studying the pasty black contents. What the hell was this anyway?

"I haven't had to deal with a witch since Kayla."

"I don't think it's the fact she's a witch that has you so frazzled. I think it's because you have feelings for her."

"Maybe," Julian admitted, then glanced at Andre through his lashes. "And you?"

"I don't have a problem admitting I have feelings for her."

Julian sighed. "This is a hell of a mess."

"It is what we make it. You know that. We can make it hard or easy. Take your pick."

"What's easy?"

"Sharing her. It's the only option." Andre shrugged. "Besides, I really don't want to have to kill you in order to have her all to myself."

Fighting a grin, Julian stepped forward and gripped Andre's chin with his thumb and forefinger. Andre didn't back away; he never did. Instead, he stood immobile, waiting. Tilting Andre's chin up, Julian brought his mouth close to his own.

"As if you could," Julian whispered and then softly brushed his lips across his friend's before catching Andre's lower lip in a playful nip.

Andre smiled. "So we're sharing her then?"

Julian chuckled and turned to walk in the same direction Addison had. "So long as I don't take a notion to kill you and have her all to myself."

"You're real funny, Julian," Andre playfully grumbled as he followed along behind him. "Was that kiss your idea of an apology?"

Julian glanced over his shoulder and snickered. "Would you have preferred more?"

"I would have preferred to hear you say it. You never actually say you're sorry."

"My God," Julian said with a chuckle as he came to a full stop. Turning, he faced his friend in surprise. "You sound like a damn woman."

Andre rolled his eyes and brushed past him.

"All right." Julian relented, spreading his arms. "I'm sorry. Happy?"

"You're kidding, right?" Andre asked with sarcasm and kept going down the hall.

Julian followed with a frown. "When the hell did this become an actual relationship, Andre?"

"Since we both began to fall in love with the same woman."

He wasn't quite sure what to say to that. Was he falling in love with Addison? God help him if he was.

He still held the cup in his hand and he raised it to study the paste. He sniffed it, then made a face at the horrid smell. What the hell kind of gift was this? He didn't know what to make of Addison. She was beautiful, feisty, but at the moment, incredibly emotional.

Her emotional roller coaster wasn't her fault. The closer she came to ascension, the less of a problem that would be. He could well remember his own ragged emotions right after changing over. Even his son Marcus had gone through something similar, but since he wasn't full-blooded, his had not been as extreme as Addison's.

No one knew for certain why some half-breeds became full-blooded vampires and some did not.

Does the why really matter?

Keeping her out of Vlad's hands was most important, until she made it through the ascension, and then they could flush the traitors out and end this, once and for all.

And then what? Will the three of us go on to live happily ever after?

Julian snorted.

There's no such thing.

Julian found Andre and Addison in the den, both standing by the window overlooking the darkened garden. He liked the way she looked in those jeans, the way they hugged her hips and accentuated her curvy, hourglass shape. He liked her figure, her long hair, and even her stubborn streak. She could handle him physically; she'd already proven that with the way her body had accepted his large cock, but could she handle him emotionally?

God knew he could be an ass. He'd proven that numerous times already. The last thing he wanted to do was hurt her or be hurt himself.

Neither acknowledged him as he came into the room, so he relented and spoke first. "Addison."

She turned to look at him but didn't speak.

He held up the cup and smiled slightly. "What do I do with this?"

Addison glanced at Andre and then turned back to Julian, hesitancy shining in her eyes. "It's a spell," she replied, her voice soft in the large room.

He took a step closer. "I kind of gathered that. But what is it for?"

"Do you really want to know?"

"I know I was an ass earlier, and I'm sorry."

Her eyes widened slightly. "I'm sorry too...for not telling you where I was going."

He tipped the cup. "I really do want to know what it does."

"It will allow you to see a sunrise."

He stood shocked, his heart racing wildly at the idea of seeing the sun again. "Are you serious?"

She nodded, and again his heart jerked in excitement.

"How?"

"It will repress your vampire traits for a short time, allowing you to be outside during the day."

"For how long?" he whispered.

She shrugged. "I'm not sure. The length of time it will last is based on your age. The older you are, the shorter time frame you'll have."

"Holy shit," Andre murmured.

"How can this little bit of paste do that?" Julian asked with trepidation.

Magic was powerful, black magic even more so, but he'd never heard of a spell that would allow him to experience sunlight. Did he dare hope she was telling the truth?

"It has to be put in your bloodstream."

"Through a cut?" Julian asked.

She nodded. "It only takes a drop."

"Why did you do this?" he asked.

She shrugged one shoulder. "Honestly, I don't know. I just wanted to."

"Why are you questioning this, Julian?" Andre asked.

"It's been so long since I've seen a sunrise, I can't help but question it. I can't imagine that it would be possible."

Addison stepped forward and took the cup from his grasp before resting her fingers against his forearm. Her hand looked so small next to his arm, so fragile, and he couldn't stop staring at it until her soft voice caught his attention.

"You keep telling me to trust you. Could you not, just this once, trust me?"

Julian nodded, almost reluctantly. She smiled and turned back to Andre, her hand still resting against his arm. "I need a knife," she said.

Andre came forward and pulled a pocketknife from his pants. "Will this do?" he asked, holding the small, thin blade up for her inspection.

She nodded and took Julian's wrist in her hand and turned it so the underside of his arm faced up. Andre pierced the skin with the tip, and a thin line of red blood ran down Julian's arm. Addison's breathing changed almost instantly. He could feel the tension coiled inside her as she watched the blood trickle across his skin. She blinked and took a deep breath, fighting her desire to taste it. He knew that battle well. It was one he'd fought every day for the last eight hundred years.

She regained control of herself and Julian smiled slightly at her strength. She was getting better, stronger. She took the knife from Andre and dipped the tip into the paste. Using that same knife, she wiped the paste across the cut, where it melted into the open wound. Instantly, he felt the change within him, the mortal weakness, the cold in the air surrounding him. Part of him tensed at the now-unusual sensations, but another part wanted to weep for what he'd lost so long ago, what he never allowed himself to miss.

Addison repeated the procedure on her own arm and he frowned slightly in surprise.

She caught his stare and shrugged. "I've been feeling a need to avoid the sun. I thought it would be a good idea, just in case."

"You haven't fully turned. It would be uncomfortable, but you would have been fine for a while."

"It's better to be safe than sorry. After all, you said yourself my transformation was moving must faster than you anticipated. I'm already feeding. I haven't been out in the sun since I arrived. How do we know for sure?"

Julian nodded and turned his gaze out the window and toward the ever-brightening horizon. Did he dare trust this? His heart hammered in his chest at the idea of standing in the sunlight for the first time in eight hundred years. He had no doubt he would risk it, even for just a few seconds.

Pushing past Addison and Andre, he opened the French doors and stepped outside. The cool air ruffled his shirt and he drew in a deep breath. He swore he could feel the morning dew as it landed on his skin, cooling his flesh. The fragrant morning glories surrounded him as they opened to greet the rising sun.

Slashes of yellow and blue decorated the sky as the sun made its first peek over the mountaintops in the distance. He smiled as the heat splashed across his face but had to close his eyes briefly against the brightness of the morning sun.

God, it had been so long since he'd felt this. Tears gathered behind his eyes as the beauty of it overwhelmed him.

"Julian?" Andre whispered as he came to stand behind him, his hands gently gripping his shoulders. "How are you?"

Julian opened his eyes and gazed at the wondrous morning sky. "Amazed," he murmured.

He felt Andre's lips press against the back of his head, but he couldn't turn away from the sunrise. Addison wrapped her arms around his elbow, and he held them against his side. Her head rested against his upper arm and he smiled, leaning down to lay his cheek against the top of her head.

"Thank you, Addison."

"This was as much for me as it was you," she said. "I had to see it one last time. It's amazing how much we take for granted. How many times in the past have I watched this, but not truly seen it?"

"I know." Julian sighed. "I did the same thing when I was human."

"How long should we stay out here?" Andre asked.

"Until the last possible second," Julian replied.

Turning, he pulled Andre to stand next to him. With a grin, Julian wrapped his arm around Andre's shoulders and hugged him close before turning his gaze back to the sky.

"Aren't you tired?" Andre asked.

Julian's lips spread into a full smile. "No. Surprisingly, not a bit."

Usually, his strength waned with the rising of the sun. He could traverse continents and, as long as he stayed in the night, could remain awake for a full thirty-two hours before fatigue finally caught up to him. Even in the dark, his body would eventually need sleep. But right now sleep was the last thing on his mind.

Chapter Nine

"Julian?" Marcus shouted from behind them, and they all turned to look. If it had been any other time, the horrified look on Marcus's face would have been quite comical. Addison fought a smile as Marcus rushed toward his father.

"What the hell are you doing?" Marcus snapped.

Julian grinned slightly. "Enjoying the sunrise."

Marcus stopped dead in his tracks, gaping at his father in such a way it made Addison laugh.

"I cast a spell," she offered.

"You performed black magic, you mean," Marcus replied.

Addison frowned. "I don't know black magic."

"Where did you get the spell?"

"From one of the books in the lab."

"Most all of those books are full of black magic, Addison. Besides, black magic is the only thing that will allow a full vampire to stand in the sunlight." His gaze shifted back to his father. "How long have you been out here?"

"Since the sun came up."

"Amazing," Marcus murmured, his lips quirking in amusement. "You never let me do anything concerning magic. You hated it."

"Still do."

"Yet here you are…"

Julian shrugged. "It was an offer I couldn't pass up."

His voice lowered and his gaze took on an amazed, almost-dreamy appearance, making Addison glad she'd done it, despite the fact black magic was frowned on by the council. He glanced up at the sky, his lips spreading into a full-blown smile so beautiful Addison felt like swooning.

The drug had suppressed his traits, but not his beauty. He was apparently this gorgeous before he became a vampire, not just after. Even she felt more normal than she had in days.

"I haven't seen this in years, Marcus. I couldn't say no, despite where it came from." Pulling his gaze back to his son, he asked, "What are you doing here, anyway?"

Marcus shook his head. "I thought Andre could use some help. I brought several men with me to help guard the perimeter."

Turning slightly, he waved his hand toward the row of about fifteen men standing on the veranda. One tall man with cold, piercing eyes watched Addison in a way that made her weary. For some reason she couldn't quite grasp, the man made her feel unsafe. Should she say something to Julian?

She turned to look at him and watched the way he studied the men. Did he feel it too? Or was it just her imagination?

"Are you sure about them?" Julian asked as his eyes narrowed slightly in distrust.

"As sure as I can be about anyone at the moment. Things are starting to shift. Word is getting out about Sebastian."

"Surely there won't be a lot of people siding with him," Addison said, concern beginning to form knots in her stomach.

"You'd be surprised, Addison," Julian replied, then sighed as his hand came to rest over hers. His fingers were warm and comforting, and she suddenly had an overwhelming urge to move closer, to better feel his strength surround her.

Andre gave Julian's shoulder a squeeze. "Why don't you stay here with Addison and I'll go with Marcus to get everyone in place and on a rotation schedule?"

Julian nodded his agreement but remained quiet as they watched him walk away with Marcus.

"I think we gave Marcus quite a scare," she said, trying to find at least a little humor in the situation.

Julian grunted, then spun around to face her. He appeared so different in the sunlight. His eyes glowed with an excitement she hadn't seen in him, and it made her heart jerk. He looked so handsome with his black hair reflecting the sunshine. His eyes squinted slightly from the glare as he watched her, and she suddenly became uncomfortable.

"Thank you," he whispered.

He brought his hand up and gently brushed her cheek with the backs of his fingers. Her skin tingled from the touch.

"You said that already."

She stopped, unable to speak past the ball of desire almost choking her. Where had this raging lust come from so suddenly? What was wrong with her?

All she knew is that she wanted him to kiss her. She wanted to feel his lips against hers, his hands all over her flesh.

"I'm not sure at the moment I could say it enough."

She smiled briefly before it faded. Licking her lips, she took a deep breath to settle her unusually rattled nerves. His head dipped, and she drew in a sharp breath, waiting anxiously for his lips to touch hers. Remembering the men, she backed away slightly and glanced toward the now-empty veranda.

"The men," she murmured.

She grinned wickedly as she walked backward, tugging him with her toward the open field past the garden. "Besides, if you're kissing me, you can't fully enjoy this."

She let go of his hand and spread her arms wide, smiling up at the early morning sky. Julian's laughter filled the air around her and her smile widened.

* * *

Sorel stood back, watching the young woman. She didn't look like her father at all, so he assumed she took after her mother. Looks wouldn't matter anyway, for what they needed her for.

He would have to be careful. Getting inside hadn't been easy, and it wasn't over yet. He needed to watch her, remain close, and hopefully, catch her alone. Sorel knew he didn't stand a chance against Julian, so he didn't dare try to take her with him around. That would be beyond foolish, but eventually, she would be alone and then he could strike.

* * *

Julian strolled through the gardens with Addison, enjoying the feel of the sun on his face. He had no idea how much time he had, and he didn't want to waste one second of it. As he strolled, an unusual sensation came over him, centering in the pit of his stomach. He stopped dead in his tracks as the unfamiliar suddenly became familiar again.

"Son of a bitch," he murmured. "I'm hungry."

"What?" Addison asked with a chuckle.

"I'm hungry." He turned to stare at Addison with wide eyes.

"Do you mean for food?"

"I guess," he replied with a frown. "It's been so damn long since I've needed to eat anything, I'm not sure."

"Try this."

Addison held out her hand and Julian watched as a piece of chocolate appeared in her palm. Julian winced slightly and shook his head. "Can't you do any better than that?"

She chuckled, the most adorable sound he'd heard in years, and popped the piece of chocolate into her own mouth. As she chewed, the expression on her face morphed into that of total bliss. Closing her eyes, she moaned as she chewed, making Julian think of wild sex, and his cock responded in kind.

Unable to resist, he cupped the back of her head and tugged her toward him. His lips slanted across hers, stealing her moans as his tongue slipped inside to get a taste of the sweet chocolate she'd just devoured.

Addison sagged against Julian as his other hand snaked around the small of her back, holding her to him. God, he could kiss. His tongue was like magic, stealing the very breath from her lungs as his mouth played her like a damn fiddle. She growled deep in her throat, her fingers fisting in his shirt as she rode out the wild waves of passion that threatened to consume her very soul.

"So," she whispered against his lips as he pulled away slightly. "Was that better than the chocolate?"

He chuckled softly and it caused his chest to brush against her already-overly sensitive nipples.

"Much better. Matter of fact," he murmured as his lips brushed across hers, "I think I'll have another."

His lips parted hers, this time kissing her slowly, gently. His mouth played with hers, softly teasing before sliding his tongue inside to explore. Addison could hardly breathe. Her hunger for him, her desire, her need, had not diminished with the disappearance of her vampire traits. It was still just as strong, still just as consuming.

He lifted both hands to cup her cheeks, holding her as he continued the sensual onslaught. Her arms snaked around his waist, her palms sliding up his strong, hard back, enjoying the feel of the muscular planes as they rippled beneath her fingers.

"Are you still hungry?" she murmured as his lips moved to her neck and nipped playfully at the sensitive flesh beneath her ear.

"Oh, yes. But not so much for food anymore."

Gripping her ass, he lifted her so her pussy rested against his hard cock. She squealed, wrapping her arms around his neck to regain her balance.

"Oh, I see what you're hungry for," she murmured, a wicked grin tugging at her lips as she shifted her pussy over his rock-hard bulge, her legs lifting to encircle his waist.

"You're going to be the death of me, angel. In more ways than one," he growled as he quickly strolled to a table nestled beneath a shade tree at the edge of the garden.

"And here I thought you were already dead," she teased.

He snorted as he set her on the table, her legs still spread, his cock nestled right where he wanted it. "So did I," he growled before capturing her mouth in another soul-stealing kiss.

Using all the concentration she could muster in her fuddled mind, she silently said the magic words to remove all their clothing. She suddenly had an overwhelming desire to feel his flesh against hers. To feel the heat of his skin and the thickness of his cock against her aching mound.

"I think I may have to change my mind about this magic of yours," Julian murmured as he dipped his head and licked his tongue across her sensitive nipple.

Addison moaned, arching her back toward his mouth as she fell back onto the table. Julian followed, his lips blazing a trail down her stomach to her now-incredibly wet pussy. His touch was like heaven, his lips like fire as they teased her flesh, sending her need for him soaring.

"Julian." She panted, almost desperate now for the feel of him inside her.

A shadow passed over her and she opened her eyes, then stared into Andre's passion-filled expression.

"Surely you're not fucking without me," he teased playfully before leaning down to gently suckle at her breasts.

Addison moaned, her whole body on fire for more. Julian's mouth moved between her legs and she groaned, lifting her hips against his face as his tongue slowly swiped along her clit.

"You're a wild little thing, aren't you, sweetheart?" Andre purred as his fingers tugged and massaged her breasts and swollen nipples.

"Please," she whispered, her hips blindly lifting to seek a more firm touch from Julian.

A thin sheen of sweat began to form along her skin as the sun's warmth added to the heat already searing her flesh. Every part of her felt like molten lava as images ran through her mind. Images and needs she never imaged she could ever feel or want. Her pussy leaked cream between the cheeks of her ass as she imagined one of them taking her there. Her anus muscle clenched and her pussy walls spasmed, so desperate for relief—relief she knew only they could give her.

"Please," she said again, this time louder.

"Please, she says," Andre teased. "What do you suppose it is she wants, Julian?"

"The same thing I do, I would imagine. Come here, Andre, and see how good she tastes."

Addison watched in stunned fascination as Julian stood between her legs and pulled Andre toward him. Their mouths touched, their tongues mated as she watched, and her desire rose a notch. Andre groaned, gripping Julian's hair to hold him close as he appeared to dominate the kiss toward the end.

Breaking away, he licked his tongue around Julian's lips. Julian studied her from the corner of his eye before pulling away from Andre and then leaning down to softly kiss the undersides of her breasts.

"Are you ready for me, Addison?" he asked softly as his lips moved upward toward her neck.

His hard cock rocked gently against her pussy, making her squirm.

"Yes." She panted, thrusting her hips in such a way as to try to make his cock go inside her desperate channel.

"Are you ready for both of us?" he asked, and she hesitated only a second before answering him.

"Yes."

His mouth covered hers just as his hips shifted. He thrust his cock inside her slowly, teasing her as his girth stretched her, filled her, giving her all she needed. They both moaned, neither knowing where one ended and the other began. He pressed forward, filling her balls-deep before grinding himself against her clit, sending sparks shooting behind her closed eyelids.

He teased her for a few moments before gently pulling out.

"No," she hissed, trying to pull him back to her.

"Shhh," he replied as he gripped her fingers and tugged her up. "Stand up and turn around."

Julian watched the tiny frown crease her brow and smiled. She did as he asked, then watched expectantly over her shoulder as he used his palm to gently press her shoulders forward. Andre stood next to them, naked, silently watching, eagerly awaiting his opportunity. Julian almost felt like denying him. He wanted Addison all to himself, but he also knew that's not how this would work. They both wanted her, and she wanted both of them.

Holding her hips steady, he slowly thrust his cock into her pussy. He closed his eyes, moaning as her wet heat wrapped around him like a glove. She was so tight, so hot, he could easily lose himself inside her. The sunlight glistened off the thin sheen of sweat covering her flesh, and he ran his palm along the gentle rise of her hips. He took a few moments to enjoy the feel of her pussy as it hungrily sucked at his cock, deliberately not thinking about Andre or anything other than how right this felt.

Addison moaned, dropping her head to the table as he slowly drew his cock in and out. Andre used his palm to pump his cock, his eyes glowing with lust and growing agitation. Using the pad of his thumb, he gently spread the cream from her pussy around the opening to her anus. He pressed forward gently, filling her ass with his thumb, and she gave a startled gasp.

He stopped. Watching her closely, he began to move his thumb in and out along with his cock. She sighed, moving her hips in time with his thrusts.

"I'm going to take you here, angel," Julian whispered, and she murmured incoherently, her head nodding in agreement.

Barely able to control his own patience, Julian pulled from her pussy and repositioned his cock at the tight rosebud opening. Spreading her ass cheeks, he pressed his cock into her, growling as her anus gripped his bulging rod tightly.

She whimpered at first, then relaxed as he pressed balls-deep, filling her. Wrapping his arms around her, he pulled her up, nestling her back against his chest. Andre came to stand in front of her, and she lifted her legs to wrap them around his waist. It was all the encouragement he needed, and Julian watched as Andre slanted his mouth across hers, sliding his tongue between her parted lips and swallowing her moans of delight.

Julian could hardly keep still. She felt so good, and every undulation of her hips against Andre's cock was driving him insane. The heat of the sun, the heat of her body, both seemed as though they were burning him alive, tearing his soul apart.

He shifted his hands to cup her breasts. They were full and firm, her nipples hard little nubs against his palms. The tiny little mewling sounds coming from deep in her throat were making his balls tighten with the need to spill his seed, to give her every part of him.

Vaguely he noticed the rising desire to bite, to sink his teeth into her neck and mark her as his, to claim her as his, but he ignored it. Pushing that nagging feeling aside, he began to move inside her. She cried out, breaking from Andre's kiss to throw her head back, staring up at the blue sky.

Andre moved his hips, positioning his cock at the entrance to Addison's dripping pussy. With a low growl, he pressed forward, thrusting deep, and she screamed, her cries filling his ears and the sky above them.

"Oh, God," Andre growled as he began to move in time with Julian's thrusts.

Julian couldn't speak. He could hardly breathe. "That's it, angel," he whispered, holding tight to the tiny wildcat as she undulated and squirmed between them.

"Julian," she moaned. "Andre. Please, I need more. I need more."

They increased their thrusts, going deeper, harder, faster. She kept up with them, panting and whimpering for more. Julian closed his eyes, burying his face in her neck and gently sucking at the salty flesh. Andre nibbled at her lips, encouraging her with softly whispered words of endearment. Julian's fingers tightened around her breasts as the need in his balls intensified and possessiveness raged through him. She was his, damn it—his.

With a growl, he thrust harder, faster, giving her everything he had. She cried out as her release hit and Julian ground his teeth as her anal muscles contracted around his cock, milking it. With a shout, he came, Andre seconds behind him. It was all he could do to hold on to her, to keep them all from falling as the three of them found their release together, the moans and shouts mingling in the sunshine around them.

As they floated from the high, Julian began to notice the burning of his flesh and winced. Quickly, the burn became almost unbearable and he pulled from her ass to fall on the ground at her feet.

Andre held Addison tight as he looked over her shoulder at Julian doubled over on the ground. Pain raced throughout his entire body and his only thought was, this is what it must be like to die.

"Julian!" Andre yelled, though Julian barely heard him over the racking pain. "Addison, get him inside now."

"Oh my God!" she screamed. "Julian."

Addison closed her eyes, willing them back to the castle and the safety of Julian's darkened room. He fell back on the bed, his skin red and feverish, his eyes tightly closed. She jumped onto the bed beside him, her heart racing at what could have almost happened, the amazing sex completely forgotten in her worry for the vampire.

"Julian," she whispered as she cupped his face. "Julian, answer me."

"I'm okay," he croaked, and she dropped her forehead to his chest in relief.

"Okay," Andre snapped as he paced the floor by the bed. "No more damn outdoor excursions."

"It was worth it, Andre. In more ways than one."

Addison watched as his facial muscles relaxed, and he fell into a deep, rejuvenating sleep.

Addison felt like crying and took a deep breath to keep her voice from breaking as she spoke. "Oh, God. What was I thinking? I almost killed him."

"He's fine, Addy," Andre said as he rubbed the back of her head. "Whatever rejuvenation he needs, he'll get while he sleeps."

She glanced up at Andre, worry still tightening her chest. "Should we stay with him?"

"We can if you wish."

He smiled slightly and brushed her cheek with the backs of his fingers. A tiny spark of jealousy shone in his gaze before he turned away from her to walk to the other side of the bed. Was he really jealous? Or was it just a trick of the light—a momentary trick of her own mind brought on by what they'd just done? She'd never had sex with two men at once. She never imagined how incredibly pleasurable it could be. She frowned and turned to look at Julian asleep. Or just how incredibly confusing.

Letting her hands fall from Julian's cheeks, Addison brushed them across his smooth chest as it rose and fell with his slow, even breathing. He still felt warm. "Should we…wipe him down with a cool cloth or something?" she asked. "He's still so hot."

"How are *you*, Addy?"

"I'm okay," she answered without looking up at him. She couldn't for some reason. Embarrassment, uncertainty, confusion…all those emotions tumbled around inside her making her feel like a rag doll being tossed around in a clothes dryer.

"Addy," he chastised as he gripped her chin, forcing her to meet his concerned gaze. "Julian will be fine. He heals when he sleeps. Right now, I'm more concerned about you. Things ended a little abruptly out there." She pulled away, licking her lips nervously. "And I know you've never done that."

"I haven't," she said, then sighed. "You and Julian are used to this. You do it all the time."

"Yes, but not with you."

Her head jerked up and she frowned at him. "What do you mean not with me? What exactly are you saying, Andre?"

"I'm saying that this time was different."

"How?"

"I think you know how."

She held her hands up, stopping him from going any further. "I don't want to have this discussion right now, Andre. I've got enough on my plate with my father trying to kidnap me and all," she said more sarcastically than she'd really meant to. Standing, she headed to the bathroom. "I'm going to go take a shower."

Andre watched her go with a thoughtful frown, then glanced down at Julian. Using the tip of his finger, he brushed Julian's hair back from his cheek, lightly touching his skin. He was still hot.

"We have a hell of a mess on our hands, don't we, Julian?" Andre whispered. "I was jealous. I've never been jealous. I'm not sure what to do about it." With a sigh, he slid his fingers through Julian's long hair, enjoying the feel of it as it feathered across the back of his hand. "I don't like you touching her," Andre added in an even-softer whisper. "And I have a feeling you feel the same about me."

Chapter Ten

Julian awoke slowly, his mind still groggy from the day before. He could still feel the heat of the sun, the way Addison's body cradled his cock. Julian frowned. He could also remember the raging jealousy at the sight of Andre kissing her.

Opening his eyes, he found the object of his thoughts lying on his side, watching him. Head propped on his hand, Andre's eyes sparkled with their usual humor.

"It's about time you decided to join us, sleeping beauty."

Julian scowled as a pounding began behind his forehead. "Why do I feel as though I just went on a massive bender?"

"Almost combusting into ashes probably has a little to do with that."

Through squinting eyes, Julian glanced around the empty room. "Where's Addison?"

"Avoiding us."

Julian's head jerked around and he stared at his friend in surprise. "She's what?"

"She slept here most of the night, although it was a restless sleep. She tossed and turned. I think she may have even dreamed of her father again, but I couldn't get her to talk about it."

Julian sat up, sighing as the pounding began to slowly ease. "Where is she now?"

"She's in the lab just down the hall."

"Alone?"

"No. Marcus and Tonya are with her." Julian nodded in relief. "Julian, we need to talk," Andre added.

"About?" he asked as he stood to stretch. Every part of him felt tight and sore as though he'd been through hell and back. Vaguely he wondered if it was the sunlight or the aftereffects of the spell.

"About Addison."

Somehow, he knew this had been coming. He turned to look at his friend. They'd been close for a long time. They'd shared many things, talked about many things, but could they share a love? Could they both love the same woman and not have jealousy tear them apart?

Julian frowned. When did he decide he loved Addison?

Andre studied him, then asked, "Was there something you wanted to say?"

"What do you want me to say, Andre?"

"What are we going to do about this?"

"About what?"

Andre sat up and scowled. "What the hell do you mean about what? What the hell do you think I'm talking about, Julian? I'm in love with her."

Julian gritted his teeth.

"Well?" Andre demanded.

"Well what?" Julian snapped.

Andre stood and walked to stand directly in front of Julian. "I'm in love with her," he repeated.

"If you're trying to get around to asking me to step aside, you can forget it."

Andre scowled. "I assume that's your way of saying you're in love with her also?" he replied sarcastically.

Julian snorted. "You know what they say about people who assume."

"Kiss my ass," Andre snapped. "I'm trying to make this work for all of us, Julian."

Julian's anger began to rise. "And just how the hell do you think this is going to work?"

"I don't know," Andre growled. "We've never been in this situation before."

With a soft groan, Julian brushed his hair back from his face and strolled to the other side of the room, trying to put some distance between him and his friend. "I don't know how I feel about her, Andre."

"But you feel something?"

Julian let out a tired sigh. "I feel something."

"So there's no chance that you'll sacrifice yourself to see me happy?"

Stunned, Julian turned to glare at his friend, then immediately noticed the spark of mischief in his eyes. Andre was teasing, trying to lighten the mood with his unusual humor. With a snort, he decided to play along.

"What about my happiness? If I recall, I'm the one that's had his heart broken."

Andre shrugged. "All the more reason for you to continue to wallow in your misery and self-pity."

"I do not wallow," Julian grumbled. "We'll work this out somehow, Andre."

"Work what out?" Addison asked from the doorway, and Julian spun around to stare at her.

She looked surprisingly adorable and composed. Her hair was braided at the back of her neck, a few tiny tendrils hanging loose around her ears. The red sweater suited her complexion and highlighted the rose in her cheeks. The way she stared at him, though, had him thinking of ripping those clothes off her again.

Her gaze wandered down his chest and stomach, and he felt his cock respond to the heat in her gaze. With a half grin, he winked at Andre. "All it takes is a look."

Addison rolled her eyes. "Fine. Don't answer my question. Your son wants to see you upstairs. Although I think he would probably prefer you be dressed when you come up there."

She turned to leave the room and Julian chuckled. "Killjoy," he called out, then laughed when she raised her middle finger, flipping him the bird.

"It's good to see you laugh, Julian," Andre said with a soft smile.

Julian nodded, but his smile faded.

They had to work this out.

* * *

Addison stood back and smiled as Marcus placed a quick kiss on his wife's cheek. Tonya smiled up at him adoringly and Marcus winked. They were so cute together, so obviously happy. What would it be like to love like that?

Her smile faded as she thought of Julian and Andre. She had feelings for both of them, but did they go beyond lust? And what if they did? What then? Would she have to choose?

She would have to. She couldn't possibly love two men, could she? This was going to drive her insane. Why was she even worried about it anyway? It wasn't like either of them had professed their undying love for her. Besides, she couldn't trust her emotions right now. One minute she was crying, the next angry. For all she knew, she could think herself in love today but hate them tomorrow.

"Good evening, all," Andre said as he strolled into the room, a broad smile on his face. He took Tonya's hands in his and kissed the backs of her fingers. "You look beautiful as always, my dear. Now how do I look?"

Tonya laughed. "You look impeccable as always, you crazy loon."

Addison smiled with agreement. Andre did look quite incredible with his black slacks and white button-down shirt. It was partly open, showing off his chest sprinkled with white hair. A black belt encircled his lean waist, and she felt the heat of a blush move over her cheeks as she remembered what impressive body part lay just below that belt.

"And you," Andre purred as he turned to face Addison, tipping her chin up with his finger. "You look perfect."

Addison smiled, feeling perfect whenever he gazed at her like that. Andre was so sweet, so tender. He made her feel special, cherished. Any woman would be crazy about him, especially if he turned on the charm. And right now he oozed charm.

"You should behave yourself in front of company," Tonya teased.

Andre grinned and turned to face her, dropping his hand from Addison's face. "But where's the fun in that?"

Addison missed his touch almost instantly and for some reason desperately wanted it back. Leaning forward, she wrapped her arms around his elbow and leaned into him. "Andre wouldn't have a clue how to behave himself."

"Now that, I would believe," Marcus said with a snicker, studying the two of them with curiosity.

Andre grinned. "What is this? Pick-on-Andre day? Even your father is in on it, if his attitude this evening is any indication."

"I don't give you any more hell than you deserve," Julian replied as he strolled into the room, looking as handsome as ever.

His gaze landed on her and Andre, and for a split second she could have sworn she saw a hint of pain, then a flare of possessiveness. She suddenly had the desire to step away from Andre, but Andre placed his hand over hers, holding her to him as though he sensed her need to flee.

Her gaze slid to Marcus, whose curiosity had obviously increased as his stare moved from his father to them. He raised an eyebrow and she shrugged slightly, unsure what more to do. Part of her thrilled with the idea that Julian might be jealous. That meant she was possibly more to him than just someone to protect or a quick fuck.

Julian's gaze locked on hers, the shadow once darkening his eyes passed, and in its place was a slight spark of mischief that made him appear so sexy. He strolled closer and she couldn't take her eyes off him as he stopped in front of her and leaned down. His lips gently brushed across hers with the barest touch that wasn't nearly enough.

"Good evening, angel," he whispered.

He smiled slightly at what must have been a stunned expression on her face before straightening and heading to take a seat at one of the stools at the kitchen island.

"What did you want to talk to me about, Marcus?" he asked in his usual brash manner.

Marcus still stood there stunned, a small smile playing at his lips. "Well, perhaps we should start with what the hell this is," he replied, waving his hand toward Addison.

"Perhaps not. Next question."

Addison snickered, pressing her lips together to try to keep from laughing at Julian's remark.

"You may not want to talk about it, but I bet I can get some information out of this one." Tonya grabbed Addison's hand and began pulling her from the room. "If the three of you will excuse us."

Addison couldn't help but grin at Tonya's pulling her from the room and into the den just off the kitchen. She plopped down on the leather sofa in front of the fireplace, pulling Addison with her. "Okay, while they're otherwise occupied. Dish."

With a laugh, Addison grabbed a small throw pillow and wrapped her arms around it, hugging it close. "God. I don't even know where to start."

"Well. Let's start with how you are."

"Confused."

"That's understandable. What about the change?"

Addison cringed. "I've been feeding from Andre. It's beginning to get easier; either that, or I'm just getting more used to it."

Tonya smiled slightly, putting Addison a little more at ease. "Have you ever fed?" Addison asked.

"Only from Marcus, but it's different for me. I don't experience the same hunger that you do. For us it's more of a...sex thing. A way of bonding, I guess. Marcus says that every vampire will feel the need to bite his mate."

"Even if she's a vampire as well?"

"Yes." Tonya hesitated, studying her. "Has Julian bitten you?"

Addison shook her head. "No." After a moment of silence, she asked. "Do you think he wants to?"

"If that look of possessiveness he gave you in the kitchen is any indication, I would say yes."

"I didn't expect for any of this to happen," Addison whispered, staring at the fireplace and the flames flickering inside it. "I think I'm in love with both of them."

It felt good to actually say it out loud, even if it was to someone she barely knew.

"Have you met Rebecca?" Tonya asked.

"Yes."

"She has two husbands."

She jerked her head back to stare at her, wide-eyed. "What?" Addison asked, intrigued.

"I could get her to talk to you, if you want. Maybe she can help with some of the emotions of being in love with two men."

Addison shook her head. "No. I feel weird enough as it is. Andre is so sweet and funny, and Julian is so…"

"Dangerously sexual?"

"Yeah," Addison said with a sigh. "They're so different, yet both of them are so…hard to resist."

"I definitely know about hard to resist," Tonya said with a grin. "Have you met my husband?"

Addison laughed. "Yes, I have, and from what I can see, he's just like his father."

"Oh, Lord, those two are going to be the death of me. They're just like kids."

Addison grinned. "I wonder what the kids are talking about right now."

* * *

"Since when is sweet, innocent, and soft-spoken your type?" Marcus asked his father as he strolled to the refrigerator to study the contents.

"Since when does it matter to you?"

"It doesn't. I'm just curious."

"More like nosy. Besides, she's not as soft-spoken and innocent as she appears," Julian added.

Marcus stood straight and grinned at his father over the top edge of the door. "Really?"

Julian glared at his son. "Change the subject," he growled.

"Jeez, aren't you unusually touchy." Marcus looked at Andre. "You have any insight on this?"

Andre just shrugged. "I have some."

"Any you wish to share?"

"Marcus," Julian snapped.

Marcus threw up his hands. "All right. Subject changed. But seriously, Julian. She's Sebastian's daughter. Does she know you used to fuck her father?"

Julian dropped his head in his hands. "Yes, Marcus. She knows," he grumbled.

"Wow." Marcus whistled as he twisted the top of the bottle of beer he'd pulled from the fridge.

"Again, Marcus," Julian grumbled as he lifted his head. "What did you want to talk to me about?"

"Rebecca has a bad feeling."

"That's it? Just a bad feeling?"

Marcus raised an eyebrow but said nothing. Julian sighed. Rebecca was one of the few witches who also had psychic ability. Although she never had specific visions, everyone knew to trust her bad feelings.

"Great," Julian mumbled.

"Should we be doing something?" Andre asked.

"Like what?" Julian asked with growing agitation. "We don't know anything specific."

Marcus stared at him in surprise. "Did you not get your nap or something?"

"What?" Julian snapped.

Marcus set his beer on the counter. "What are you so pissed off about?"

"He's pissed at me," Andre replied from his spot still leaning against the cabinets on the far side of the room.

"I'm not pissed at you!" he yelled, unsure why he was mad himself.

"You're pissed at somebody," Marcus said.

"I'm pissed off at Sebastian. I don't know why the damn son of a bitch just can't stay dead."

Marcus chuckled and Julian sent him a glare that would have silenced most men, but his son just ignored it. Leaning forward, Marcus put his hands on the counter. "What's really going on, Julian? Are you in love with Addison?"

"I'm worried about Addison. I'm worried about all of us."

"So am I, but that's not what's going on with you."

"What's going on with me right now…and Andre," he added with a wave of his hand toward his friend, "is something Andre and I will have to work out. Right now, we need to focus on keeping Addison safe."

"Fair enough. But Dad, seriously…if you need to talk."

"I'm fine," Julian growled.

Marcus nodded, letting the subject drop.

* * *

Addison stood in the shower, letting the warm water soothe away her tension. It felt good to have a few minutes of time alone to just think. Last night had been rough. She'd dreamed of her father, lain awake for hours thinking about Julian and Andre, and of course, remembering that amazing time outside. Just thinking about it now made her body feel alive and warm.

The drug still ran through her veins. She could tell because the hunger had been less intense. So much so, she could ignore it and remember what it felt like to be human again.

Closing her eyes, she raised her hands to cup her breasts, weighing them in her hands. Soapy, her hands slid easily over her flesh, and she sighed, wondering how just imagining the three of them together could make her so hot for them so fast.

As the water splashed over her skin, the now-familiar pang of hunger began to grow in her gut. She cringed, fighting hard to keep the sensation at bay for just a little while longer. She hated this. She hated the feeling, the hunger, the need. Sharp pain sliced through her stomach, and she gasped, reaching out to steady herself against the wall. For some reason, it was so much worse this time.

She screamed as another sharp pain racked her body, and she slumped back against the wall, panting for breath.

"Addison!" Andre yelled as he came into the bathroom, Julian close on his heels.

They threw open the shower curtain, and Addison looked up at them, tears in her eyes. "What's happening to me?" Cringing, she growled her way through another slicing pain that felt as though it were cutting her in two.

Julian pushed Andre aside and bent down to pick her up in his arms. "It's going to be okay, angel," he murmured as she wrapped her arms around his neck, trying to breathe through the pain.

"It'll pass, just breathe."

"I can't." She panted. "I've never felt anything this bad in my life."

"What the hell is going on, Julian?" Andre demanded, the anxiety in his voice obvious.

"Because of that spell, she hasn't fed in a while. Her body is starting the shutdown."

"Shutdown?" he asked.

"She needs to feed. Andre," Julian commanded, then turned to look at him as he laid her on the bed, "give her your arm."

Andre rolled up his sleeve, preparing to offer himself.

Addison squealed as another round of pain cut through her middle. Her heart then sped up, jumping in her chest like it might try to burst free. Andre sat on the bed next to her and placed his bare arm in front of her lips. She squeezed her eyes closed, not wanting to, yet at the same time instinctively knowing it would make everything better.

She leaned forward, licking at his flesh before sinking her fangs into his arm. Andre hissed, then bent to place gentle kisses against her temple as she fed.

"Does it help?" he asked.

She nodded as the pain ebbed and the all-too-familiar feeling of euphoria took over. But with the feeling of euphoria came the lust.

Her pussy clenched and she released Andre's arm, leaning her head back against Andre's shoulder. Julian's hands gently pushed her thighs apart. He watched her closely as his palms slid up the insides of her legs. She licked her lips, anxiously awaiting the touch of hands against the very part of her that ached the most. Even her ass craved the thickness of their cocks, both of them filling her, pleasuring her.

Cream leaked from her pussy as Andre slid his hand down her stomach to cup her labia. His gently massaging fingers made her squirm and buck against his hand. Lower they slid until they found the tight rosebud opening to her anus and one finger pressed forward into the tight hole. Addison moaned, her hips lifting off the bed in wild abandon.

Julian moved over her, his mouth toying with her breasts. She gasped, burying her hands in his hair to pull him closer. He reached up and pushed her hand back down, planting it firmly in the mattress beside her hip. Holding her wrist, he continued his sensual onslaught against her nipples, flicking his tongue back and forth over the engorged nubs. She groaned, arching her back as both men drove her wild with need.

Andre's hand moved back to her pussy where two fingers thrust deep, fucking her with long, slow movements. But it wasn't enough. Her entire body felt on fire. She needed more. She needed them.

"Oh God," she moaned, struggling to retain control but at the same time struggling to lose it. "I need you."

"I know you do, angel," Julian whispered against her lips, his hot breath teasing her mouth as his tongue traced her parted lips. "And we need you...I need you," he added, just barely loud enough for her to hear.

Her heart skipped a beat. Between them, Andre's hand moved to free Julian's cock from his pants. She watched, enthralled, as Andre ran his palm up and down Julian's thick rod with slow, sure movements. Julian moaned, closing his eyes as he placed small, nibbling kisses along her jaw.

"Fuck her, Julian," Andre murmured.

Julian lifted her legs, wrapping them around his waist as he positioned his throbbing cock at her weeping entrance. She could hardly wait and lifted her hips against him, forcing him halfway inside before he could stop himself. He hissed, holding himself still as she struggled to accommodate his girth.

"That's it, sweetheart," Andre whispered. "Take all of him."

His hand slid between them to toy with her clit, and she cried out, bucking her hips wildly. Julian pulled back, then thrust forward hard, pinning Andre's hand between them as he pressed as deep as he could go, filling her with his thick heat.

Addison was close…so close. Every part of her thumped with life, lust, and hunger. Julian pulled back so that Andre could move his hand, then he gripped her hips, pulling her upward as he fell back. She landed on top, his cock impossibly deep, and she moaned her pleasure, finding a more comfortable position and riding him hard. His hands were everywhere, holding her up, squeezing her breasts, forcing her to take even more of him as he thrust his hips upward.

Andre came around in front of her, placing his massive cock before her hungry lips. She opened her mouth and then engulfed his length. He tasted of musk and salt, smelled of heaven and male.

"Oh, I like that, Addy," he purred as she ran her tongue along the thick vein on the underside of his cock.

She did it again, twirling her tongue around the tip, licking at the precum that had escaped the small opening. Julian gripped her hips, moving them back and forth, rocking her against him. He moaned, pressing upward as she rocked, sending her senses skyrocketing every time he put pressure on her clit.

Using her hands, she gripped one of Andre's thighs, while with the other she massaged his balls, toying with them gently as she licked at him like he was her favorite piece of candy, not able to get enough.

Andre let out a breath, digging his fingers into her hair. "Keep that up and I'm going to explode."

"I want you to explode," she murmured, then engulfed him into her mouth. Relaxing her throat, she took him as deep as she could, swallowing and running her tongue along his length. Through her half-opened lids, she watched him, unable to take her gaze away as he closed his eyes in pure rapture.

His cock throbbed along her tongue and she sucked hard, enjoying the soft, velvety feel of his flesh. The hairs at the base of his cock tickled her nose, and she pulled back slightly, her teeth scraping at his length along the way.

Andre gasped, his hips jerking forward, his hands holding her head steady as he fucked her mouth. Julian's hands moved up her rib cage, holding her upward, supporting her as Andre lost himself down her throat with a shout. His warm, salty cum filled her mouth, and she swallowed all of it. Using the pad of her thumb, she stopped the stream of cum dripping down the underside of his cock, then used her tongue to swipe it clean. Andre shuddered and she smiled.

"We're not finished," Julian murmured, then pressed his hips upward, forcing his cock deeper and making her gasp in surprise.

"How do you want it, angel?" he asked, rocking his hips.

"Harder," she whispered.

Andre moved and Julian rolled them over, putting her on her back. Moving to his knees, he lifted her legs around his waist, put his hands on the mattress by her shoulders. She braced herself, waiting eagerly for what she so desperately needed. And he gave it to her with one long, hard thrust.

She screamed, her fingers clenching in the fabric of the bedspread as he pounded into her over and over, harder and deeper, until she thought she'd die from the building pleasure racking every one of her limbs.

"More." She panted. "More."

Julian gripped her hips with one hand, holding her still as he pistoned harder, grinding against her clit every time he went deep. She cried out, moving her hips with him, taking everything he gave her.

"Yes," she squealed as her release barreled through her womb.

Her pussy spasmed, squeezing at his cock, begging for more. Julian came with her, his hips working against hers, pushing himself deeper into her core until she thought he would split her in two.

With a sigh, he dropped his forehead to hers briefly before rolling to his side and pulling her with him. She felt like a rag doll, unable to move. Truthfully, she wasn't even sure she wanted to move.

The heat from Andre's chest seeped into her cold back as he pressed against her, pinning her between him and Julian. She'd never felt as safe as she did now, so protected. Or so damn confused. They both gave her everything she ever needed, but could they remain this way?

A prickle of awareness snaked down her spine, and she stiffened, raising her head slightly to glance around the room. She suddenly had a sick feeling they weren't alone.

"I sense it too," Julian said softly. "Be still."

She lay back down, her body now tense and nervous. Her fingers curled against Julian's chest as she tried to snuggle just a tad bit closer. Had whoever it was been watching them all this time? She shuddered at the thought, and Julian brushed his hand up her arm, soothing her. Andre kissed the back of her head, holding her closer.

"Who is it?" she whispered.

"I don't know."

"It has to be a wizard," Andre offered. "Whoever it is, is using magic."

"What makes you think it's a male?" Addison asked softly.

"It's a male," Julian replied. "Trust me on this."

The sensation disappeared and Addison let out a sigh of relief. Sitting up, she glanced around the room, studying the darkened corners. "Why would someone be watching us?" she demanded.

"He's waiting for his opportunity," Julian replied as he stood. "Stay with her, I'm going to talk to Marcus."

Addison watched him go and almost chuckled. "Julian," she called, and he turned to face her, his eyebrow raised in question. With a wave of her hand, she dressed him in the clothes he wore earlier. "I think your son may take you a little more seriously if you're dressed."

* * *

Sorel stood in his room, squinting his eyes shut as the pain in his balls became almost unbearable. He certainly hadn't expected to see that erotic display. Watching Addison fuck the two of them had driven him damn near insane.

She'd been in the shower alone. It would have been his perfect opportunity, but he'd waited too long enjoying the view of her naked flesh. And when she'd begun to play with her own breasts, all thoughts of kidnapping fled.

He needed to stop lusting and start planning. She was very seldom alone so he would have to be on his toes. The right moment would probably only be a window of a few seconds. Not much time at all.

They only had a few more days left. Time was of the essence, and he could not fail.

Chapter Eleven

Julian quickly made his way to the den. Strolling through the doors, he found his son on the couch, kissing Tonya. He cleared his throat, getting their attention, although he almost hated to break it up. He enjoyed seeing his son as happy as he was. Tonya had been good for him. She loved him.

Marcus pulled away and glared at him, making Julian's lips twitch in amusement. "What?" Marcus snapped.

Tonya slapped him on the chest and Julian smiled, but it quickly faded. "You have centuries to fool around; right now I need your help."

Sitting up straighter, Marcus looked at him, his brow creased in concern. "With what?"

"Someone was just in my room."

"Did you see who it was?"

"No. I just sensed them. Addison did as well."

"They used magic," Tonya murmured.

"Can you find out who?" Julian asked.

Marcus shook his head. "No. He has to actually be casting the spell at the time. It works like tracing a phone call."

"Damn," Julian growled, his anger at this whole mess growing.

There was no doubt Addison was getting stronger, but she was still nowhere near ready. Once she turned, she would be at her strongest, but even then it was doubtful she could take them on her own. It was now obvious Vlad not only had vampires on his side, but wizards as well. Apparently Sebastian wasn't the only wizard who felt making an alliance with the vampires would be a benefit. Only Sebastian had taken it a step further and become one himself. If he'd only known then what a sick ass the man was.

"Could it be one of the men who are here?" Julian asked.

"Truthfully, it could be anybody, Julian. If powerful enough, whoever cast that spell could be thousands of miles away. There's just no way to know."

"Damn it," he snarled.

Julian picked up a glass on the end table and threw it. The glass shattered against the wall, splashing its contents all over the paneling and hardwood floor.

"I wasn't finished with that," Marcus drawled.

Julian turned to glare at him. "Then pour yourself another! This is fucking ridiculous. Why the hell can't you find Vlad?"

Marcus stood, facing him head-on. "Julian, you need to relax. Blowing a gasket isn't going to help matters. Nicholas and Darien are doing the best they can. Their uncle Vincent arrived yesterday to lend a hand. They will find him."

Julian snorted. "When do you think? Before or after he gets his hands on her?"

"I think this is getting just a little personal to you."

"Don't start analyzing me, damn it! Yes. I'm worried about her, Marcus. A blood rite will probably kill her."

And if that happens, it will kill me.

* * *

Addison strolled through the darkened garden, watching the full moon cast its white glow across the manicured lawn. This protected dimension was quite an interesting place. Everything ran on its own. There were no gardeners, no housekeepers; the castle literally ran itself.

Of course, it would, she thought to herself. The place was created by witches and wizards. It was a place of magic, and at times, mayhem. With that thought, she remembered the time in the garden and shivered slightly as tingles ran down her spine. It had been perfect, just like this place, and part of that bothered her. This place wasn't real, so could the emotions she felt be not real, as well?

Behind her, Andre coughed softly, and she turned to stare at her two ever-present sentinel guards, Julian and Andre. Julian stood tall, broad, proud, but in his gaze was just a hint of worry that in turn made her worry. Andre stood next to him, his stance just as proud, just as tall, but in his gaze she noticed the usual mischief replaced with concern.

"The two of you are following me around like puppies," she said, trying to lighten the mood just a little.

"We can't leave you alone," Julian replied, not even a hint of amusement in his voice.

Addison sighed. "I haven't felt that presence anymore."

"That doesn't mean he's not here."

"Is it so bad having us around?" Andre asked, one side of his mouth tilting up slightly.

"Of course not," she answered. "It's just weird now. With you following me around like you are, it makes the whole danger thing that much more real."

Julian's voice was a bit harsh when he spoke, surprising Addison. "It needs to be real, Addison."

She frowned. "Did something else happen that you're not telling me?"

"No," Julian replied.

"Do we have any idea at all who it might have been?" she asked, referring to the presence from earlier.

"The only thing we know is that it was a wizard," Julian replied. "Let's talk about something else."

She blinked, wondering what he had in mind. "Okay. What about?"

He licked his lips, glancing away toward a bench not far from the path they walked along. "Let's go sit there."

With a questioning glance toward Andre, who shrugged in response, she turned to follow Julian. He looked tired, drained.

"How long has it been since you've fed, Julian?" she asked.

He glanced at her over his shoulder before turning his stare back in front of him as he made his way across the grass. "I fed in France."

"That was several days ago. Shouldn't you feed again?"

"I can go many more days than you can, Addison. I'm fine."

"Well, let's be real here," she grumbled sarcastically. "Everybody can go longer than me. I can't seem to even go a full twenty-four hours without needing more."

"That's what I wanted to talk to you about." He reached the bench and dropped down on one side, making room for her next to him. Andre continued to stand, his arms crossed over his chest as he watched them. "You can't keep feeding off Andre."

"Oh," she breathed. "Okay."

"Julian, I'm fine," Andre argued, but Julian put up his hand, stopping him.

"I need you at one hundred percent. If she's feeding off you, you won't be."

Addison shook her head. "Wait. I don't want to have sex with a bunch of strangers just so I can feed."

"You won't have to."

"Then how?"

"We'll trance them."

"Trance them?" she asked with a scowl. "Like you did to me that first day at Marcus's."

"Yes."

Addison swallowed nervously as she remembered all the other times she'd fed. "I want sex after I feed."

Andre looked as though he was about to say something, but again, Julian stopped him. "We'll come straight back to the castle and take care of that here."

"Take care of it?" she snapped, her anger beginning to rise.

"Obviously, that didn't come out quite right," Andre murmured.

Julian scowled up at him. "Shut up."

"God, what is with you two lately?" Addison stood and glared down at Julian. "For starters, I'm not something that has to be 'taken care of.' Secondly, who died and made you lord and master? Isn't this something we should all be deciding together, not just agreeing to whatever you come up with?"

Julian stood as well, standing over her with his usual dominant attitude, and it took a lot of strength on her part not to back down. Instead, she lifted her chin in defiance.

"That's not what I meant, Addison, and you know it. As for lord and master, yes, I am. Andre isn't a vampire, and as of yet, neither are you, so both of you are going to have to trust me on the feeding issue. You need to feed, and you're not going to do it from him." Raising his hand, he pointed toward Andre. "We both need him at his best."

Addison ground her teeth, for some strange, childish reason wanting to fight him on this. It just didn't feel right. Maybe she'd just become too comfortable feeding off Andre. She shifted, torn between standing her ground and fleeing.

"This is ridiculous," she ground, her jaw tightly clenched.

"No, this is important." Julian stepped forward and cupped her chin, forcing her to meet his beautiful blue gaze. "I know this is all strange to you, and I know…" She tried to pull away, but he held her tight, forcing her gaze back to his. "I know this is going to be hard. You've become accustomed to Andre." He smiled slightly at his friend, who stood close by, before turning back to Addison. "I also know Andre feels possessive right now and doesn't want to share you. But both of you need to trust me on this."

She glanced toward Andre and his lips twitched. She partly smiled back, but her heart just wasn't in it. She didn't want to feed from anyone else. God, it felt like cheating. Andre gave her a small nod of encouragement, but it didn't really make things better.

"Will he at least be there?"

Julian sighed and dropped his hand from her chin, then gave her a small nod of assent. "If that's what you want."

"I don't know what the hell I want. I want to be normal. I want to be someone else's daughter. I want this over already!"

"I know," Julian whispered.

He gathered her in his arms, hugging her close. She wrapped her arms around his waist and rested her head against his chest. The slow, steady beat of his heart was somewhat soothing. On the back of her head, she felt Andre's touch as his fingers gently combed through her hair.

"I know something else I want," she whispered.

"What's that?" Julian asked.

"I want the two of you to kiss and make up. Stop fighting over whatever it is you're fighting over."

"How do you know we're fighting?"

She didn't miss the hint of amusement in Julian's voice, and it made her stomach flip. "If you think I've missed the heated glares when you think I'm not looking, you're mistaken."

Andre chuckled.

"What are you fighting over anyway?"

"You," Julian replied.

She tilted her head back to look up at him. "Me? Why?"

"Just leave it at that for now," he whispered.

Leave it at that? What the hell was that supposed to mean?

She glanced at Andre and he just smiled. "I concur with Julian on this one."

"Now you do." She dropped her hands from around Julian's waist and slapped at Andre's arm, making him chuckle. "That figures. But you still haven't kissed and made up."

"I have an idea," Andre said as he grabbed her hand and pulled her closer. "I say we all kiss and make up."

His mouth slanted across hers, causing the butterflies in her stomach to do flips. His lips were warm and soft, so gentle and coaxing, every part of her responded. When his tongue dipped inside her mouth, she moaned in pleasure, enjoying the taste of him. Even his smell invaded her senses, making her weak with growing need.

Behind her, she felt Julian tug at her hand, pulling her away from Andre.

"It's my turn," he whispered, and he tipped her chin up with his finger, bringing her mouth to his.

Julian's kiss was completely different from Andre's. It was demanding and bold where Andre's was gentle and seductive. He was definitely the alpha. Everything about him screamed alpha, and it made her want to fall to her knees in submission.

His lips played over hers; his tongue forced its way inside, demanding a response. Andre still held her other hand, and he brought her fingers to his mouth, gently sucking on them one by one as Julian continued to plunder her lips and drive her need to a fevered pitch.

Pulling away, he turned toward Andre and gripped his chin. Addison watched as Julian pulled Andre toward him, his mouth descending on his hungrily. Andre responded in kind, his lips parting to accept Julian's tongue, his moan of pleasure getting lost in the kiss.

Addison couldn't get over what watching them did to her. To see them kiss didn't take away from their masculinity; it added to it, gave it a note of dark sexuality and need. It was wild, and it made her wanton and definitely more brazen.

Grasping a handful of each of their shirts, she tugged, pulling them apart.

"Kiss me like that," she murmured as she lifted on her toes to kiss Julian.

He did just that, devouring her mouth like a man starved. She whimpered, hardly able to breathe as his tongue danced around hers, teasing her. After a few seconds, she pulled away and tugged at Andre's shirt.

She didn't have a moment to say anything before Andre slanted his lips across hers in a kiss no less demanding. It surprised her that the usually gentle Andre could be this...wild. The kiss was amazing, robbing her of breath and thought, making her think of only one thing—getting them inside her.

Every part of her burned with a need she wasn't sure she would be able to control. Julian cupped her chin, pulling her away from Andre and back to his mouth. It was like a game of sensual tug-of-war, going back and forth between the two of them, losing a little more of herself with each kiss.

Andre moved behind her, his hands coming around to unbutton her top. His hands cupped her breasts through her bra and she moaned, arching her back toward his palms. His hands slid lower, pushing her bra up and over her breasts, exposing them to the night air and the ministrations of his fingers. Long, graceful fingers tugged and pinched at her nipples.

Her fingers fisted in Julian's shirt and her nails scraped at his flesh through the material. Anything she might have wanted to say was swallowed by Julian's kiss...that demanding, soul-shattering kiss that had her writhing like a wanton slut.

Warm, soft lips nibbled at the side of her neck as Andre moved his hands lower and into the waistband of her pants. She whimpered, grinding her hips back against him as he slid lower, ever closer to that part of her that was literally on fire.

"I want to feel your pussy," he whispered in her ear just as his fingers moved between her legs, cupping her aching mound. He hummed his approval as her hips moved with his hand's gentle massaging.

"You're so wet, sweetheart," he purred as his fingers separated her wet slit, smearing her cream around her clit and opening.

Her legs began to tremble, and she leaned back against him, her hands still holding tight to Julian.

"That feels so good," she whispered against Julian's mouth.

"That's only the beginning."

Julian reached down and unfastened her pants, shoving them down her hips. Bending, he removed her shoes and pulled her pants free, exposing her pussy to the night air and a second set of hands. She moaned loudly, sighing toward the night sky as they both slid two fingers deep into her channel.

On his knees before her, Julian licked at her clit and her hips bucked, wanting more. My God, she wanted so much more. The two of them moved in counterpoint, teasing her with shallow thrusts before both of them thrust both sets of fingers deep, pushing her to her toes as she cried out into the night.

"Please, one of you," she murmured. "One of you, fuck me."

"Just one?" Andre whispered.

"No," she sighed. "Oh no. I need you both. Please."

Andre used one hand to free his thick cock. From behind her, he slid it between her legs, teasing her opening with slow, gentle glides along her slit. Julian was still on his knees in front of her and raised his hand to rub along Andre's cock as he teased Addison.

She gasped at the erotic image, unable to take her gaze away as Julian licked at the head of Andre's cock as it pressed forward to rub against her clit. Addison ground her hips, rubbing them against Andre's long, thick cock as Julian pressed upward with his palm, putting pressure against both of them.

She could hardly take it anymore. She wanted that cock inside her...now. "Andre," she groaned, bending slightly, trying to force his cock inside her.

He gave her what she wanted, thrusting deep enough to steal the very breath from her lungs. Julian licked at her clit, moaning as her juices dripped out, coating his chin and Andre's balls. Grabbing him at the base, Julian pulled him free of her pussy.

Addison whined, wanting him back inside her until she looked down and saw Julian engulf the tip of Andre's cock in his mouth, licking her cream from the head. It was erotic and sexy, and she couldn't turn away.

Andre groaned before pulling away and sliding his cock back inside her aching walls. Addison gasped as he began a slow, deep fuck, thrusting three times before pulling back out again.

"Damn it, no!" she yelled, blindly reaching between her legs to grab his cock and force him back inside.

Julian grasped her hand in his and stood. He walked backward, pulling her with him toward the bench. "Get rid of our clothes, Addison," he commanded, and with an impatient wave of her hand, all their clothes as well as hers disappeared.

She wanted them so badly her legs shook as she walked the few feet to the bench. Julian sat, straddling the concrete. In her impatience to have him, she shoved him back against the bench. His smile encouraged her to continue, although she knew she would have anyway. She was beyond reason now, beyond any common sense. Her only coherent thought was that of sex—wild, steamy sex.

Pressing her hand against his chest to hold him down, she straddled his hips, placing her pussy just over his bulging cock.

"Take it, angel," he ground out and pressed his hips upward.

With a moan, she shifted, putting the head of his cock at her weeping entrance, and slid down, taking every inch of him into her throbbing channel. She screamed as his girth stretched her, filled her. Julian's hands moved up to cup her breasts, squeezing and molding, holding her upright as she undulated her hips against him, her grinding motions forcing him even deeper.

Andre moved in behind her, pressing against her back until she rested against Julian's chest. The new position put much-desired pressure on her clit, and she whimpered, shifting slightly for more friction, which sent shards of pleasure down her spine.

"Do you have any idea how beautiful you look when you fuck him?" Andre purred, his soft French accent playing havoc with her senses.

His long fingers moved to her pussy from behind, stroking through the cream as it leaked from her walls. With slow, gentle strokes, he moved to her ass, smearing the juices around the tight rosebud entrance before sliding his fingers inside to mimic Julian's thrusts.

The added pressure to the sensitive walls of her pussy from the other side sent every part of her into orbit. She was so close. Every muscle trembled; every inch of her felt on fire. The need that began to center in that dark spot terrified her and at the same time fed her desire, igniting it even higher.

"Andre," she groaned, almost desperate now for the pleasure the two of them could give her.

"Do you want me?" he purred, thrusting his fingers in and out, stretching her tight anus with scissorlike movements that made her gasp. "Do you want me here?"

"Yes, damn it, yes!" she cried, barely able to hold back any longer.

She could feel the pressure building in her womb, the blood pounding through her veins as well as theirs. Three hearts beat in unison as Andre shifted over her and Julian and thrust his cock deep into her ass.

She winced slightly until the sharp bite of pain subsided and the pleasurable fullness took over. Both of them began to move, thrusting together, each whispering words of encouragement, some she didn't even understand. And truthfully, she didn't care. All she cared about was the sensations, the feel of them inside her, their hands as they stroked her flesh, their lips as they kissed her brow, shoulders, and neck. Nothing else existed but this.

"Oh God," she moaned as her womb spasmed, sending shock waves throughout her body and theirs.

"Fuck," Julian moaned more than once as her pussy squeezed and milked his cock for more. "She's going to come, and I'm going to fucking explode."

"So am I," Andre purred. "Addy, I'm going to explode all in this heavenly ass of yours. Come for us."

Addison moaned, her body no longer controllable as she bucked and wiggled between them. Julian gripped her hips, holding her still as he and Andre increased their thrusts, pumping into her harder and deeper.

She buried her head into Julian's chest, moaning against his skin as they drove her ever higher. From somewhere far away, she heard Julian hiss, and tasted the warm trickle of blood that pumped into her mouth as her body erupted into a million tiny pieces of utter ecstasy.

As her body eased from the high, Julian grabbed a handful of her hair and tugged harshly, pulling her neck up to his lips. With a growl, his teeth sank into her flesh, making her shudder and explode all over again. Andre gave a loud shout behind her and, with one final thrust, spilled his seed deep into her ass. Julian quickly followed, his moans lost against her neck as he fed.

Julian pulled away, his reluctant growl echoing across the garden. In shock, she stared down at his chest. Blood smeared across his pecs, seeping from the two tiny bite holes slightly to the right of his heart.

"Oh my God. I bit you," she whispered.

"Close it, angel," Julian said with a sigh.

She glanced at his face. His eyes were closed, his lips slightly parted and coated with blood. She reached up and wiped at her neck with her fingers, shocked to see the blood coating them. It had been her blood. He'd bitten her.

"It's okay, Addy," Andre soothed from behind her. "Lick his chest and close the wounds."

Swallowing, she leaned forward and licked her tongue across the wounds. The warm, spicy taste of his blood made her shudder, but she fought the rising need for more. Julian lifted up as well, then ran his tongue along her neck to close hers. It was an unusually erotic sensation that sent goose bumps across her skin.

Was this what Tonya had been talking about? Was this the need to bite your mate?

"Ah, angel," Julian purred. "You're killing me. I can feel you getting aroused again. I can feel your pussy getting wet." He shifted just a little, making her sigh and proving his point as her juices leaked out to coat his balls.

"What is it about this garden?" she murmured, placing soft kisses against his chest.

"I don't think the garden has anything to do with it," Andre replied, his voice full of amusement.

Suddenly, she felt Julian stiffen beneath her. As soon as she did, her own sixth sense kicked in, picking up that same sensation of being watched. Whoever had watched them before was back, or maybe he'd been there all along. She shuddered at the idea of someone staring at them, watching them have sex.

Andre pulled from her ass and turned to stare at the large flowering bushes not far from the bench. It would be easy for a man to hide there. Even the moonlight didn't penetrate the darkened shadows created by the plants.

Julian lifted his head, looking at Andre around Addison's shoulder. "He's back."

Sorel stood still as a stone, his hand holding tight around his cock. He'd stumbled upon them and couldn't resist watching, but apparently, they'd heard him moan when he spilled his cum. He swallowed, not even wanting to breathe as he stared straight into Andre's eyes. They knew he was here, but they couldn't see him. They could only sense him.

Damn, he should have been more careful. He should have kept his damn cock in his pants. But the sight of her taking both of them, the sounds of her cries as they pleasured her, was more than he could take, and he'd ended up doing something stupid.

He had been paying more attention to his masturbating and not enough attention to the spell, and he'd ended up almost giving himself away. What was he saying? He *had* given himself away. Thank God it was only a sound and not a visual of him standing here, cock in hand like a voyeuristic idiot.

Julian sat up, his sharp gaze scanning the bushes, the anger in his eyes glowing, sending Sorel a warning he understood well. If he ever caught him, he'd kill him. He had no doubt about that. Julian was a mean son of a bitch when pissed off.

Sorel's gaze moved to Addison. She remained on the bench, using her magic to conjure up a blanket to wrap herself in. He frowned, disappointed he'd lost the view of her curvy body, but deep down knew he needed to get out of here. He couldn't waste any more time watching them. If he kept it up, sooner or later, he'd give himself away, or Marcus would figure it out.

Don't worry, Addison. You'll be back with your father soon.

Chapter Twelve

Julian stood in his basement room, staring at the painting on the wall of home—his Romania, which he missed terribly at the moment. He could see Addison there, making the castle her own, hunting with him, sharing his nights with him.

Then, of course, there was Andre, this damn threat hanging over their heads, and this wizard they had no idea how to find.

What did he want? What was he doing? Was he biding his time?

Glancing over his shoulder, he watched Addison sleeping in the massive bed. Andre lay next to her, his arm encircling her waist and holding her close. The image made him feel torn. He loved Andre. They'd been friends for a long time—centuries—but could he share Addison with him? Share her in every way, not just sex?

Andre believed they could. He believed their deep friendship would allow them to find a way. Julian wasn't so sure. Part of him still hated seeing Andre touch her. It still tore his soul apart to watch her kiss him, to see the affection in her gaze when she looked at him.

He loved her. He knew that now. Still, nagging doubts about her father trickled through his mind. Was all this a setup? Was she really in with her father and just got caught up in their little game of protection? He dragged his hand through his hair, a tired, ragged sigh leaving his chest with a *whoosh*. Why was he having such a hard time trusting her?

"Julian." Andre spoke softly from his spot on the bed.

Julian turned to look at him. He still lay next to Addison, her fragile body cradled in his arms. For some reason he had to turn away and did, his chest tightening in jealousy.

"We need you at one hundred percent as well," Andre continued.

"I know."

"Then come get some sleep. She's restless. I think she would feel better if you were here with her."

Julian sighed, his eyes closing tight for a brief second. "She's dead to the world, Andre. I doubt she would know if I was there or not."

Addison squirmed, her knees drawing up to her chest, her voice whimpering across the room. Julian moved quickly to lay beside her and cup her heated cheeks.

"A nightmare?" Andre asked in concern as he watched them.

"Maybe. God only knows what Sebastian might be doing to her while she sleeps."

Gently, he kissed her forehead. "It's okay, angel. We're here with you."

The cold fog seeped into Addison's bones like a dull knife, cutting through her flesh as well as her defenses. She knew this feeling. She'd been here before. Straightening her spine, she hardened her resolve. She had to get through this. Julian and Andre waited for her on the other side, just beyond the fog. She could feel them, smell them.

She could also feel the danger...the evil surrounding her like a shroud. Shivering, she tried to ward it off, shake off the feeling of utter terror that threatened to consume every part of her. She could do this. She was strong enough.

Taking a deep breath, she moved forward. The fog parted around her like ripples in a lake, but as it did, its icy breath moved over her flesh, freezing her.

"It won't be long now, Addison," a voice called, and she froze, unable to move any farther.

"I won't help you."

"You have no choice in the matter."

"Yes, I do."

"This can be painless, Addison. You can agree to join with me. Rule with me and I can save you, keep you alive."

Addison shook her head. "No. I will not help you wipe out the mortal race."

"You've been listening to Julian," the voice snarled. "He'll hurt you. He's a liar. He cares only about himself. He doesn't love you, Addison. He can't love anyone."

Addison shook her head in denial, tears threatening to stream down her face. "You're the one who's lying!"

"I know him, Addison. I know how he thinks, what it is he truly wants. And I can guarantee it isn't you."

"What is it then?" she snapped. "What is it he wants?"

"He wants what he can't have. What's been dead for four hundred years. He can never love you as long as he's in love with someone else, and you know who that is, Addison."

Tears slipped past her tightly closed eyes to slide down her cheeks. He was wrong. Julian did love her; she could feel it.

"Come with me, child. I'll protect you from him. I'll keep you happy."

She shook her head.

"A blood rite doesn't have to be certain death. I have the power to keep that from happening. I can keep you alive."

Her lower lip trembled, and her arms wrapped around her waist as pain sliced through her chest. Pain at the thought of losing Julian and Andre. Pain at the thought of them getting hurt because of her.

"Julian will fight you. You know that."

"Julian is a fool and will pay for his deceit," he growled, sending shivers of apprehension up her spine.

"No," she cried. "No. I can't let you hurt him…or Andre."

"Then help me, Addison. Help your father. I promise if you do, they will not be harmed."

"I don't believe you!" she shouted toward the fog.

"I have not lied to you. Has Julian? Has Julian professed his love for you? Has either of them told you of their feelings, or have they just used your body for their own pleasure?"

Addison felt sick. Bile rose in her throat, threatening to spill out on the path at her feet. She knew deep down Julian loved her. Didn't he? Hadn't she seen his jealousy? Hadn't she seen the caring in his gaze, felt it in his touch? Or had it all just been wishful thinking? Why was he doing this to her? Why was he making her doubt everything?

She knew why. Deep down she knew.

"I can't," she sobbed. "I can't help you do it."

"It's your choice, my child. You have time to think it over. Remember what I told you about Julian. He'll only hurt you, child."

Addison awoke with a start, her limbs shivering despite the warm bodies on either side. Her tear-filled gaze landed on Julian as he lay next to her. He appeared to be asleep, his hand resting lightly on her hip. Andre was curled behind her, his soft, even breath blowing against her hair. The sensation was comforting, and she snuggled deeper into their arms.

In the back of her mind, her father's words continued to sound, continued to feed the doubt and anxiety.

Would they hurt her as her father said?

Even so, it wasn't reason enough to help him. What he wanted was pure madness. King of a new dark world? A world of utter chaos and death where fear ruled and vampires reigned at the top of the food chain?

Fatigue muddled her thoughts as her eyelids once again grew heavy. It must still be daylight outside for she still felt the need to sleep, but part of her feared sleep—feared the dreams that plagued her when she closed her eyes. Now the doubts would plague her waking hours.

* * *

"New Orleans?" she asked, her brow raised in surprise.

Julian grinned. "Lots of drunk people that will be easy to trance."

Addison glanced around at the crowd. Mardi Gras was in full swing. Lots of people everywhere, most drunk off their asses. The sound of music carried along the breeze and would certainly cover anyone's screams... *if* they screamed.

She walked along with Julian, Andre behind them, ever watchful. The idea of feeding off a stranger wasn't sitting well with her, but she couldn't deny the hunger was beginning to grow. She'd learned to fight it off for a little while, but eventually it would literally eat her alive and she'd be withering in pain like the other night.

Out of the corner of her eye, she watched Julian. His gaze scanned the crowd and women turned their heads to stare at him. How could they not? He was gorgeous. But to be fair, Andre got his share of drooling female stares as well.

She wanted to believe they were all hers, but her father's words still continued to ring through her head like a broken record.

He'll hurt you, Addison. He only wants one thing and it isn't you.

He hadn't seemed to notice her anxiety, or if he did, he probably chalked it up to the upcoming feed. Truthfully, part of it was because of that, but most of it was because of her dream and her own nagging doubts.

They hadn't told her they loved her. They hadn't even hinted at it, but then neither had she. She'd only just realized it herself and still worried that her jumbled emotions were wrong.

God, this was going to drive her insane before it was all over!

Turning a corner, Addison almost walked right into a couple making out against the brick wall of the bar. At first, she thought they were just kissing and quickly replied, "I'm sorry, excuse me."

Her gaze wandered downward, and she noticed their hips—their grinding, undulating, naked hips.

"Oh my God," she said, moving quickly to get around them.

Her heart hammered wildly in her chest as she stole a quick look back over her shoulder at the two still wildly going at it, completely oblivious to the crowd around them. It was sick, really, but watching them made her own pussy cream and her nipples bead.

"Addison." Julian spoke softly close to her ear and she jumped, jerking her head back around to the front.

The heat of a flush moved over her cheeks and she kept looking everywhere but at Julian.

"It's pretty erotic, isn't it?" he said, the amusement in his voice obvious.

"More like shocking. I thought they were just kissing."

Andre chuckled. "Hell of a kiss."

With a swat of her hand to his chest, she grinned, some of her anxiety beginning to ease. "Stop it," she hissed playfully.

With a purely devilish smile that made her heart skip, Andre gripped her hand in his. Bringing it to his lips, he kissed her knuckles, sending warm tingles up her arm. The look in his gaze was warm, tender, and she searched desperately for anything resembling love.

Julian cleared his throat, catching their attention and breaking the mood. "We need to keep moving. I want to get this done quickly."

"Sure thing, boss," Andre grumbled, his gaze narrowing toward his friend. "But we wouldn't have to be here at all if you'd just let her feed off me."

"We've been through this already, Andre," Julian snapped as he turned to head farther down the dark street.

"Let's be honest here, Julian. This doesn't have anything at all to do with strength."

Julian turned to glare at Andre, the look in his eyes murderous, and Addison took a step back in reflex. He'd been so moody lately, so angry, and she wasn't quite sure why.

"Now is not the time to get into this," he snarled.

Andre took a step closer to Julian. Addison reached up to grab his arm and didn't miss the tension coiling his muscles. "I think we need to get into this, Julian, and the sooner the better."

"Stop it! Both of you," she hissed, moving to stand between them.

She opened her mouth to say more, but a sharp pain tightened the muscles in her stomach, and she gasped. She doubled over and Andre caught her to him.

"Find someone, Julian," he snapped. "Otherwise I'll take care of it whether you like it or not."

Julian nodded. "Get her to the alley."

Andre picked her up in his arms. She buried her face in his neck, tears burning the backs of her eyes. My God, what would she have done if she didn't have them? How would she have survived this?

"Andre. What happens to people who turn that don't have anyone to help them?" she asked.

Andre turned down into one of the small alleys off Bourbon Street. They weren't alone. Two other couples engaged in sex lined the walls, and Addison tried her best to ignore them, but she couldn't block out the sounds, the moans, the grunts, the cries of ecstasy. She could even smell it in the air. The scent of sweaty bodies, cum, and sex. It was all too much, and her skin began to burn.

"If they don't have anyone to help them, they become a slave to the hunger. Feeding indiscriminately, taking too much, never understanding how to control it. Those usually don't last long."

"Why?"

"They're killed by other vampires."

"Why?" she asked again, her breathing becoming more and more ragged.

"Because they're too dangerous. To the other vampires and to themselves."

She swallowed and shifted against his chest, pressing her nipples against his hard muscles. Her arms snaked around his neck, her fingers digging into his soft white hair. She felt her fangs descend and moaned as the need to taste him burned through her veins.

"Deep breaths, Addy," he whispered.

"I'm trying," she murmured and snaked her hand into his shirt, sifting her fingers through the hair covering his chest.

Another pain tightened her stomach and she winced, praying she could keep this under control, praying she didn't lose it and attack Andre. His neck was so close, his blood so close.

"Julian will be here soon."

"Why is he so mad at you?" she asked, trying to think of anything but the hunger, the heat of his body, and the sound of his heartbeat so close to hers.

"It's complicated, Addy," he whispered.

"Is it me?"

Andre's chest rose and fell with his deep sigh, but he said nothing.

"Andre," she whined, sounding almost desperate as her fingers brushed across his nipple.

"I can't speak for him, Addy."

"But you know why he's mad?"

"Yes," Andre hissed as she pinched at his hard nipple. "Addy, you have to stop that or I'm going to fuck you right here."

"I can hear them…fucking…grunting," she groaned as another pain sliced through her body. "I can even smell them."

"Ignore it."

"I can't. It hurts, Andre. The hunger, the need. It actually hurts," she sobbed.

"I know," he soothed. "Damn it, Julian. Where the hell are you?"

* * *

Julian stood on the sidewalk of Bourbon Street, scanning the crowd for someone…anyone to give to Addison. He'd dismissed men. A woman would be much easier. Besides, he didn't like the thought of giving her a man.

This was so not what he needed. He'd never in his life been this jealous, or even jealous at all, and he hated the feeling. He needed to brush it aside and focus on getting her a victim. She needed blood and soon.

Across the narrow street an attractive young woman waved to him and smiled. Julian grinned back, narrowing his stare on the woman as he crooked his finger. Her smile widened as she crossed the street, her walk sexy, her short dress meant to tease and seduce. She appeared to be alone, so that was perfect.

"Hello," she purred.

She raised her hand to touch his chest, then ran her painted nails along the buttons of his shirt.

"Hello," he replied back.

Her glassy gaze left no doubt to him she was at least a little drunk, which would work in his favor. The less she remembered the better.

"Come with me," he commanded, and she smiled, putting her hand in his.

He kept his gaze on hers as he brought her fingers to his lips and kissed the backs of them. He could hear her strong and steady heartbeat, smell the blood in her veins, and his own heated with need. He would feed later. Right now, he needed to take care of Addison.

Her eyes widened slightly just before she swooned drunkenly into his arms. He caught her easily, helping her steady herself against his side. To anyone around them, it would just appear as though she were too drunk to walk alone. She whimpered something as they turned into the alley where Andre and Addison awaited him.

Andre set Addison on her feet facing him. She stared at him with a questioning expression...one filled with concern and a slight flare of jealousy.

"A woman?" she asked, panting now.

Julian moved the girl in front of him, supporting her back against his chest. Gripping her hands, he wrapped them around her middle, holding her immobile. The young woman moaned, moving her hips against his cock, but Julian only had eyes for Addison. The woman's movements did nothing for him.

"The woman was easier," he murmured, then pulled the woman's long brown hair to the side, exposing the side of her neck, all the while keeping his gaze on Addison.

She licked her lips, her wide stare immediately moving to the pulse rapidly beating against the woman's skin. Julian nodded as Andre gripped Addison's wrists, lifting her hands to rest against the woman's waist.

Addison leaned forward, touching her lips to the woman's neck while Julian slid his hand up the woman's skirt. She didn't wear panties, so it made it easy for him to find her clit and stroke it through the folds of her wet pussy.

"Oh, kinky," the woman moaned, and giggled drunkenly, her hips undulating against his hand.

Addison's lips parted, baring her teeth.

"Easy," Julian murmured softly, and she took a deep breath before sinking her teeth into the woman's flesh.

The woman flinched, then moaned in pleasure as Addison fed almost greedily. She came against Julian's hand, her moans mingling with the others in the alley. To anyone looking, it would just appear as a kinky foursome, nothing more.

"Not too much, Addison," Julian said softly, and she pulled away, her gaze wild as she stared at him over the woman's shoulder, the woman now limp in his arms.

Addison's breathing was ragged, and he knew what she needed now. Unfortunately, he couldn't be the one to give it to her. It would have to be Andre, and that tore his chest apart.

"Take her home, Andre," he whispered. "I'll take care of the woman. Addison, can you use your magic?"

She nodded, her eyes half closed, blood still lingering on her lips. Her small hand reached out to touch his. "Come with us."

"I can't. I have to take care of her. I'll be there soon."

With a nod, he lifted the woman in his arms and stepped to block the view of Andre and Addison as they disappeared from the alley. With a sigh, he glanced down at the woman in his arms.

"What do you do when you and your best friend are in love with the same woman?" She mumbled an incoherent response and Julian snorted. "You don't have the answer any more than I do."

* * *

The second they were back at the castle, Addison jumped Andre. Wrapping her arms around his neck, she slanted her lips across his, her tongue demanding entrance.

Andre moaned, returning her kiss in kind as his arms wrapped around the small of her back, holding her close. Her beaded nipples pressed against his hard chest and she moaned, anxious for the feel of him without clothes.

Just as the thought ran through her mind, she absently waved her hand, unclothing both of them.

Andre's heat seeped into her flesh, warming her. The euphoria from the feed still pumped through her veins as she tried not to think about what Julian might be doing. Was he feeding from the woman? A pang of jealousy made her stomach lurch, and she held tighter to Andre, exploring his mouth like a woman starved.

He tasted of mint and raspberries with a hint of the coffee he had earlier. Even his musky smell sent her senses reeling, but what really made her wild was the feel of his mouth on hers, the way his teeth nipped at her lips, and the way his hardening cock pressed into her stomach, grinding hungrily.

God, she wanted him…needed him with everything she had in her. His hands moved lower to cup her ass and lift her against him. Her legs wrapped around his waist, her pussy nestled perfectly against his long, thick cock. She groaned, sliding her labia along his shaft.

He moaned, grinding his hips with her, his kisses swallowing her mumbled pleas to take her, to put her out of her misery and make her come.

As he moved across the room, every step he took made his cock slide enticingly against her clit. She broke away from his kiss and buried her face in his neck, inhaling his scent. Her fingers curled into his back, leaving half-moons on his flesh as she fought for control.

"I need you, Andre," she sighed, wiggling her pussy against his length.

He stopped midstride and forcibly set her away from him. "Not yet, damn it. It's probably one of the only times I'll have you alone, and I'm not going to rush it."

Picking her up by the waist, he tossed her the final two feet to the bed, where she landed on her back with a squeal. Andre strolled to the foot of the bed, his heated gaze taking in every inch of her burning flesh. Addison held her breath, every inch of her throbbing for his touch.

With one hand, he gripped her ankle, pressing it back to bend her knee. She smiled coyly as he placed his lips against the inside of her ankle. Tingles ran up her leg as his lips gently worked a path up past her knee. His palms flattened against the inside of her thighs and they fell open, exposing her wet pussy to his gaze and mouth.

Her fingers fisted in the covers beneath her as he slowly moved over her, his hot breath teasing the folds of her aching mound. Her hips lifted off the bed, seeking a firmer touch.

He used his palm to press down on her lower stomach, forcing her hips back to the bed.

"Be still," he commanded in a deep voice, sending shivers of hot lust up her spine.

She bit down hard on her lower lip, struggling to keep from shoving her pussy in his face. She'd never been an aggressive person, never been the seducer, but now she wanted desperately to do that. She was changing, becoming more alive, more in charge, more aggressive, and it thrilled her.

"Andre," she whispered, feathering her hand down her stomach. With shaking fingers, she separated her labia, exposing her sensitive clit.

"You don't take orders well, do you?" Andre said with a grin, looking up at her through his lashes.

"Is that a problem?" she teased.

"No," he said with a slight shake of his head, his lips twitching into an adorably roguish smile. "Because I know how to take care of that."

Moving upward on his knees, he straddled her hips, then gripped both her wrists in one hand. Her heart raced wildly at what he might have in mind.

"Conjure me up a couple of silk scarves, my little witch."

Addison smiled and two red silk scarves appeared on her stomach. Andre grabbed them and pressed one of her wrists to the bedposts above her head. Wrapping the scarf around her wrist, he secured it to the post.

"Can I trust you to not use your magic to get out of this?"

She nodded, her throat too dry to really speak. She never imagined this would turn her on like it did. Tied up and at his mercy did wonderful things to her body and mind.

"Good," he purred, then tied the other wrist.

Andre stared down at Addison tied to the bed, completely at his mercy, and smiled. She was so beautiful. Her face was flushed, her hair spread out on the pillow around her head like a soft halo, but this gorgeous little vixen was no angel. She was a wanton wildcat, so completely different in the bedroom than she was out of it. Her true self came out to play, and it was a beautiful sight to behold—one that left him breathless.

Sliding his hand beneath her ass, he lifted her hips. She gasped and let her legs fall to the side, exposing her pussy. Pretty, pink, and wet, it lay before him, totally his.

He leaned down, inhaling her sweet, musky scent. She sighed, lifting her hips toward his face. With a smile, he used the fingers of one hand to slide through her slit, smearing the juices that poured from her opening to coat his hand. Her moans filled the quiet of the room and made his heart pound. His cock strained to be inside her but he'd be damned if he'd rush this.

He was more okay with sharing than Julian was. Little pangs of jealousy always gripped him when he watched them together, but deep down he knew the three of them together was as it should be. Julian would eventually see it too. It would just take him a little longer. Hell, Julian was still fighting falling in love with her, but he knew his friend, knew the doubts and fears that plagued his mind and heart. Julian was tough. He'd been through hell, but Andre also knew that when he did love, he loved with everything he had in him.

He would come around. He'd see to it.

Shaking thoughts of Julian from his mind, he continued to tease and toy with Addison's pussy. Cream flowed from her opening, and he smeared it between the cheeks of her ass, smiling as she wiggled and squirmed beneath him.

God, he wanted her. Needed her. His balls ached with the need to spill their seed deep inside her. He wouldn't be able to hold off much longer. Leaning down, he licked his tongue along her slit, then wrapped his lips around her swollen clit. She groaned, bucking her hips wildly against his face. He suckled, teasing her with the tip of his tongue as he thrust two fingers deep into her wet channel.

Her cries of pleasure floated around him, wrapping around his heart and mind like a blanket of contentment. She sounded so damn sexy and tasted like heaven.

Growling, he let go of her clit, removed his fingers, then positioned himself between her thighs. He teased her opening with the head of his shaft, just barely going inside. She whimpered, lifting her hips and forcing his cock deeper inside her channel. Her warm, tight walls sucked at his cock, and he ground his teeth to keep from losing his mind.

"Say my name, Addy," he whispered against her lips.

"Andre," she whispered, and he pressed in just a little deeper before pulling almost out.

"Again," he breathed, licking her lower lip with his tongue.

"Andre," she replied, this time a little louder.

He thrust deeper but not all the way, still teasing her and himself with the slow, shallow thrusts.

"Again."

"Andre," she groaned, this time lifting her hips as he thrust deep and hard, hitting her cervix with the head of his cock.

He sighed, closing his eyes at the feel of her milking him. His balls drew up tight; his body tensed, his hands shaking, he was barely able to hold himself in check.

"Oh, fuck," he sighed.

He began to move, slow and deep at first, then hard and fast. His hips pistoned into her hungrily. Addison met every thrust, her lips crying his name with every push of his cock. Her fingers fisted into the scarves as she tugged against them, arching her back and bucking her hips wildly.

Putting his palm beneath her ass, he lifted her so he hit her clit with every pump of his shaft. She cried out, her eyes closing tightly shut as she exploded around him. Her pussy spasmed and trembled against his cock, sucking him until he too found his release, thrusting hard and spilling his seed deep inside her, giving her everything he had.

With a sigh, he dropped his forehead to hers. "I love you, Addy," he whispered. "That's why Julian is mad at me. Because I love you."

Addison remained silent, tears gathering in her eyes. He loved her? Deep down she hoped it was true, but what her father said still remained in her thoughts. Using magic, she removed the scarves and then wrapped her arms around Andre, holding him close.

I love you too, Andre. With all my heart. But I love Julian also.

What was she going to do?

* * *

Addison bent forward over the pool table, taking her anger out on the balls. Where the hell was he? It was almost dawn. Was he still with that woman?

She rolled her eyes, then hit the white ball, which struck two others knocking them into the corner pocket. She wasn't a jealous person…normally. She wasn't jealous. She was worried. That's all. Just worried.

"You're hitting those balls awfully hard," Andre called from his spot at the bar, a plate of steak and baked potatoes in front of him.

Addison had spent the first two minutes he was eating watching him. She loved steak, missed it terribly. She'd even tried taking a bite, but it had been nasty and she'd spit it out almost immediately.

"Doesn't have anything to do with Julian, does it?" he asked softly.

"I'm worried about him. What's taking him so long? He was just hiding her somewhere, right?"

"Worried he fed off her?"

"No!" she snapped. "I know he has to feed... It's just...I know he does it during sex."

"Not always, Addy."

That didn't really help her any, and she had a feeling Andre knew it. She tried to turn her attention back to the pool table.

Julian stood just outside the door listening. Was she really jealous? A small smile tugged at his lips before he turned the corner to walk into the room. At the bar sat Andre. He nodded his head in acknowledgment as he came in. Julian returned it, then kept walking toward Addison.

Just as he was about to get close, she stood straight and pressed the butt of the pool cue against his chest, stopping him. Turning, she shot him an angry glare. "Where the hell have you been?"

He glanced down at the stick pointed right at his heart, then back up at her. He couldn't stop the grin that pulled at his lips at her demeanor. She was adorable angry. Glancing over her shoulder, he didn't miss Andre's amused expression.

"Don't look at me," he replied. "I've been here all night."

Julian scrunched his nose at him before turning his attention back to Addison. With one hand, he grabbed the tip of the cue and moved it to the side, tugging gently as he did so to move her closer.

"Were you worried about me?" he asked softly.

"Yes," she replied, her gaze softening despite the anger still simmering just below the surface.

"Why were you worried about me?" he asked, wrapping his arm around her waist and pulling her close.

Raising one hand, he cupped the side of her neck, running his thumb along her cheek. Her skin was soft, her face already beginning to take on that glow of ethereal beauty all vampires possessed.

"Vlad's still out there," she whispered.

"Yes." He nodded in agreement. "But I was careful. Is that the only reason?"

She shook her head, her eyes closing for just a second before opening back. In them, he could see every emotion careening through her—fear, love, and uncertainty. She pulled away from him and tossed the pool cue onto the table where it landed with a clang against the wood trim.

"My birthday is very close," she said with a sigh. "The closer it gets the more dangerous it gets."

Julian stepped up behind her and placed his hands on her shoulders. She was tense, her shoulders tight. Raising his hands, he rubbed at them, trying to relax her.

"I've been having these awful dreams about my father." Julian tensed, but he remained silent, waiting on her to continue. "He tries to get me to go with him...to help him.

How are we going to fight him, Julian? How do we know that even if we kill him that someone else won't jump up and take his place? This battle could continue on forever."

Julian turned her to face him. He cupped her face, forcing her to look at him. "Listen to me, Addison. This will end with Sebastian's death. He can only do this once. If we kill him a second time, he will remain dead, and with his death, this movement will also die."

"How can you be certain?"

"None of us can ever be certain about anything, but I believe this will end."

"And then what?" she asked, staring into his eyes.

"That's up to you, angel." He brushed his thumb across her lower lip.

"Perhaps you should tell her how you feel before you asking her to make a choice," Andre snapped from the bar.

"She already knows how I feel."

Julian's jaw clenched as he turned to glare at his friend.

"How do you feel, Julian?" she asked softly.

He opened his mouth to tell her, but Marcus ran into the room, interrupting them. "I need to talk to you. Now."

Chapter Thirteen

"Stay here with Andre," Julian commanded, then quickly left the room with his son.

Addison sighed and slapped at her thigh, then glanced guiltily at Andre. The last thing she wanted to do was hurt his feelings, but he didn't appear hurt. Instead, he watched her with mild curiosity.

"Do the two of you really want me to choose?" she asked.

"I don't. I'm afraid I can't speak for Julian."

"What do you mean you don't?"

"I believe a threesome would work. Julian and I love each other. I love you… I'm pretty sure Julian loves you. The only question that remains is whether you love both of us or is there one of us you love more than the other?"

She stared at him in shock. "Andre, that's crazy," she murmured.

"What's crazy? That you would have to choose, or that I would suggest a threesome?"

"The threesome."

"Why?"

"How would that work?"

"If you love us both, it will work, Addy. We'll make it work."

"You don't think Julian would be okay with it, do you?"

Andre stood and walked over to the pool table. Crossing his arms over his chest, he leaned back against the table. "I sometimes see the two of you together and I get a little pang of jealousy." Andre smiled slightly. "Julian gets a big one."

She smiled wickedly. "I never get a pang of jealousy when I see you and Julian together."

Andre laughed. "It turns you on to see us kiss or touch, doesn't it?"

"Yep."

Again, he laughed, making her smile. She loved his laugh. It was deep and strong and came from way down inside him.

Addison frowned as another thought popped into her head. "What if Julian doesn't want to share?"

"Then it really will be up to you." Andre studied her for a moment, his gold-green eyes watching her closely. "Your father tells you things about Julian, doesn't he? Bad things."

She licked her lips and dropped her gaze to the floor. "Yes. He says he'll hurt me."

Andre reached out and tipped her chin back up with his finger. "Julian will never hurt you, Addy. I've known him a long time. He may be stubborn, at times cold and menacing, and always dominating and arrogant. He can even be cruel to his enemies, but I have no doubt he loves you."

"I'm glad you do," she said with a deep sigh.

"Why don't you go take a hot shower? It should help to relax you a bit."

"Yeah, maybe."

With a nod, Addison headed to her room, Andre following close behind.

* * *

"What's going on?" Julian asked as he followed Marcus into the den. The room was empty except for the two of them. "Where's your wife?"

"She went to Germany with Rebecca, albeit reluctantly."

A slight smile played at Julian's lips. "I can imagine."

"The spells are originating from inside the dimension."

That certainly got his attention. "Can you pinpoint who?"

"Not yet."

"Damn it," Julian snarled. "Get all of them out of here."

"I think it would be best if we leave them here. If we get rid of all the men, it will tip them off. As long as he doesn't know that we know, he'll do it again."

Julian dragged his hand down his face in growing agitation. "We don't have much time, Marcus."

"I know."

"If they're going to try and make a move it will be soon."

"I know."

Julian shot his son a glare.

"What? I'm agreeing with you for once."

Julian strolled to the fireplace and stared at the flames flickering within the grate. For the first time in his life, he was at a loss. He knew what would be the smartest thing to do, but he just couldn't bring himself to put Addison in that much danger.

"I think you should let them take her."

Julian blinked as his son voiced the very thought that had been running through his own mind.

* * *

"Are you out of your fucking mind?" Andre snapped, staring at Julian as though he'd lost his marbles.

"We can track her," Marcus offered. "It's our only way of finding them."

Andre came to his feet and began pacing the length of the library. "What if we don't get there in time? Or what if they block her in some way? The two of you couldn't have seriously thought this through."

"We have thought it through," Julian replied. "We've talked out every possible scenario."

"If we keep her here, once her ascension has passed, it's over."

"No. It's not," Marcus said with a sigh.

Andre stopped pacing and put his hands on his hips, glaring at Marcus. "What do you mean, no it's not?"

"I've been doing some research. He can still come back. It will be harder for him, and he won't come back fully reformed, but it can be done. Addison is his best shot, and they'll exhaust every possible chance to get her, but if they don't, it's by no means over."

"Son of a bitch! So...what? We leave her alone and wait for them to take the bait?" He narrowed his gaze at his best friend, who right now he wanted to fucking throttle.

A thought suddenly occurred to him and he growled, his whole body tensing. "When you asked me to come here, did you put that spell of protection around Addison's room so we would know if anyone went in there?"

Marcus shook his head. Andre tensed with fury. Had he misjudged Julian? How could he do this to Addison.

"You son of a bitch," Andre's snarled, then turned to leave the room, quickly heading back to Addison.

Behind him, he could hear Julian yelling at him to stop, but Andre ignored him, determined to get to Addison before anyone else did.

* * *

Warm water trickled down Addison's flesh but did nothing to soothe her. Julian still hadn't discussed his feelings with her. If anything, he'd been avoiding her. She knew how she felt about Andre. There were no doubts there. She could easily be happy with him.

But Julian.

She knew how she felt about him too, but he still kept that wall there, still held a part of himself back. That frightened her the most. She didn't want to play second fiddle to a long-dead love he couldn't let go.

A noise sounded from behind the closed bathroom door and she stood still, listening. "Julian?" she called.

She thought he'd stayed in the other room, but a sudden wave of trepidation traveled the length of her spine. Something was wrong; she could feel it deep in her gut.

Turning off the water, she grabbed a towel, keeping her gaze on the door. Once dry, she wrapped the robe around her and stepped out into the darkened room. Someone was here. She could feel his presence, hear his heartbeat.

"Who's there?"

Vlad stepped from the shadows, and Addison drew in a sharp breath of surprise. She began to back away, using her hand to feel her way along the wall, too afraid to look away from Vlad.

"What do you want?" she hissed.

"You know what I want."

"*Vorlace!*" she shouted, trying to freeze him in his tracks and allow her precious seconds to escape.

His lips spread into a smile of utter contempt as he stepped forward, grasping her by the lapels of her robe. "You've been bound, bitch."

"You can't bind me," she snarled, raising her chin in defiance.

"No, but I can," someone replied as he stepped from the shadows at the far side of the room.

Addison recognized the wizard. Not his looks, but his presence. "You're the one. The one who's been watching me." He was also the one she'd seen that first day they'd arrived…the one who'd given her the creeps as he'd watched her from the veranda.

"Yes. I'm Sorel, your father's student…of sorts." He touched her cheek with the tip of his finger, and she recoiled in disgust. "You have quite a passionate nature."

"We don't have time for this, Sorel," Vlad hissed. "Marcus will pick up on our presence any minute now."

Addison tried desperately to think of a way out of this mess. He'd bound her, which meant she wasn't able to use witchcraft, but maybe she could do something else.

Taking a deep breath for courage, she shoved hard at Vlad's chest, catching him by surprise. He fell back, letting go of her lapel, and she leaped for the bedroom door. Sorel was too fast for her and grabbed a handful of her hair. He tugged with enough strength to bring tears to her eyes, and she landed back against him with a squeal, struggling to loosen her hair from his grasp.

Where were Julian and Andre? Why had they left her here alone?

Or…

"What have you done with Julian and Andre?" she snapped.

"Why, nothing…yet," Vlad replied with a leer that made her feel ill.

Her heart raced in real fear as worry for the two men she loved ate away at her insides. The door opened and Andre burst into the room, his face a mask of absolute fury. Sorel raised his hand, sending an invisible wall that slammed into

Andre, throwing him back out the door and against the stone wall of the hallway.

She heard the sickening crack of his skull as his head hit the wall. He sank to the floor, his eyes closed, his body immobile.

"Andre!" she sobbed.

Her knees gave way and she would have collapsed onto the floor if Sorel hadn't been holding on to her hair and keeping her upright.

"It's time now, Addison, to meet your father," Vlad sneered.

* * *

Julian turned the corner of the hallway and immediately noticed Andre trying to get to his feet just outside his bedroom door. He rushed forward and gripped his elbow to help him stand.

"Get off me," Andre snarled, jerking his arm from his hand.

Julian let him go, then turned to go into the bedroom.

"They took her," Andre growled from behind him, one hand holding his bleeding head.

Julian swallowed, his own heart breaking just as much as Andre's. He hoped Andre would eventually understand, but as he looked at the hatred and anger shining in his friend's glare, he doubted it would be anytime soon, and it would be never if anything happened to Addison.

He turned his gaze to his son, silently praying this worked and they hadn't made one hell of a mistake.

"Where is she, Marcus?" he asked.

Marcus held his hand out, staring into the tiny crystal ball nestled in his palm. Smoke swirled within the crystal, changing colors from gray to blue to bloodred. His son's eyes met his over the ball, and Julian's hands fisted at his sides.

"I swear to God, Marcus..." Julian snarled, his anger and apprehension growing with his son's prolonged silence.

* * *

Vlad shoved Addison forward and she landed hard on her hands and knees at the foot of a long black coffin. She winced at the sharp bite of pain as the concrete scraped her hands and knees. Lukewarm water splashed onto her robe and hair, mixing with the tears that streamed down her face. Images of Andre's still form filled her mind. She closed her eyes, trying to pick up on his presence...anything that would let her know he was still alive. She felt nothing, and the tears increased their flow.

They were in some underground drainage system. Pipes ran along the ceiling. Some leaking, which must be where the water was coming from.

"Your father wishes to give you one last chance, Addison." Vlad spoke as he walked around the coffin to stand before her. "Join with him."

She shook her head, her gaze still on the ground where she could see her teary reflection in the shallow layer of stale water that covered the floor. "No. I'd rather die than help him."

"So be it then," Vlad snarled.

He reached down and grabbed a handful of her hair. She cried out as he pulled, forcing her to her feet. "He could save you," he hissed in her face. "He could save you, and Sorel and I could take the place of your other lovers."

She spit in his face, then braced herself for the blow she instinctively knew would come. The blow was harsh, loud, stinging as his palm landed across her cheek, temporarily blurring her vision. She gasped but otherwise remained quiet before jerking her head around to glare at him.

Vlad grinned, making her stomach knot in fear. "The blood rite will most likely not kill you, Addison." He hissed, baring his teeth. "But for that, I will. Prepare her," he yelled before throwing her to the ground.

Addison tried to scamper away on all fours but was caught and tossed to a flat concrete table next to the coffin. The cold of the concrete seeped into her back, and she shivered as her body temperature lowered. Four sets of hands held her down as she struggled against them in vain.

A sharp, piercing pain traveled up her arm as they sliced into her flesh, exposing the vein in her wrist.

"Hold her still, damn it," one of the men snarled. "I'll nick the vein if you don't."

Addison struggled harder. A loud bang permeated the air as pain burned through her midsection, taking the very breath from her lungs. Glancing down in horror, she gasped at the bleeding wound in her stomach. A coldness unlike anything she'd ever felt took over. It traveled through her veins and limbs, making it harder and harder for her to move.

"Do you have any idea what silver does to a vampire?" Sorel asked with a wicked smile as he stared down at her and waved the gun close to her nose. The smell of smoke and sulfur burned her nose, and she jerked her head away. "It renders them immobile."

Her hand fell away as her strength completely faded. Silent tears filled her eyes, and with the last bit of gumption she could muster, she shouted, "Damn all of you to hell!"

"Ah, sweetheart," Sorel murmured. Leaning close, he licked his tongue across her cheek, making her cringe in disgust. "We're going to bring hell right here to earth."

Chapter Fourteen

Addison could feel her life draining away. Regrets plagued her muddled mind. She should have told them she loved them. Now they would never know.

"Julian," she whispered. She turned her head slowly and watched as her blood traveled through the tube attached to her arm and into her father's withered body. "Andre," she murmured, becoming more tired by the second.

She had little if any time left. She had no hope. The wound in her stomach only half healed; the silver running rampant through her body added to the growing fatigue and need for sleep. As her blood drained, she became colder, but she didn't have the energy to even shiver.

The blood rite wouldn't have killed her, but Vlad had made sure she knew he would. He'd given strict orders for her to be completely drained—punishment for her spitting on him, she assumed.

Beside her, Sebastian sat up, his body filling in, his flesh taking on a healthy pink glow. Addison could only stare and silently pray it would be over soon, that Julian and Andre would be smart enough to stay away, to run and hide.

Her eyes closed. She didn't want to see him. Instead, she wanted to focus on Julian and Andre—their nights in the garden.

A loud commotion erupted behind her, and her father yelled, his anger echoing around the darkened room, mingling with the sound of a wolf's menacing growl. Addison tried to look behind her but was too weak to move her head. Someone pulled the tube from her wrist, allowing what remained of her blood to spill onto the table.

She thought she heard Julian's voice but wasn't sure, only to decide it was nothing but wishful thinking. There was nothing that could be done for her now. Even she knew that.

"Addison," Andre yelled, but his voice sounded so far away.

She turned her head, seeing only vague shadows and quickly moving images. She tried to lift her hand, but it fell lifeless to the table.

"Addison," he yelled, this time much closer.

Screams and yells sounded all around her. The sound and smell of death filled the room, almost choking her with its putrid odor. What was going on? What was happening?

She opened her eyes to see Andre's face directly in front of her. She squinted, trying to bring it more into focus, but couldn't. This couldn't be real, could it?

"Andre?" she whispered, touching his cheek with her trembling fingers.

He felt warm, soft. The noises around her still continued as more people joined in the fight. She glanced to the coffin, but her father wasn't there.

Someone wrapped her wrist, holding it tight and causing her to wince. Andre tugged her up, holding her against his chest as he positioned his wrist at her mouth.

"No," she sighed, shaking her head and pushing his arm away. "No. I won't help you."

"Addison, it's me, Andre." When she turned her head away again, he whispered, "Addy, please."

She still wasn't sure what was happening. Was this really Andre trying to help her? How did they find her? Or was it just a hallucination—a trick of her dying mind?

Again, he placed his wrist before her lips. Warm blood trickled into her mouth and she opened her lips wider, wrapping them around his wrist to suck greedily. She couldn't get enough and continued to drink the warm, spicy fluid. It warmed her body, sharpened her mind.

Through her lashes, she could see the battle going on around her. The men fighting, the vampires feeding. They were everywhere. Her stare caught Julian at the far side of the room and her heart jerked. He fought with another vampire, but just a few feet away, her father raised a crossbow, aiming it right at Julian's back.

She let go of Andre's wrist and it fell to her lap, lifeless. Everything seemed to happen in slow motion as she grasped Andre's cold, lifeless hand and screamed, "No!"

* * *

Julian heard her scream and shifted in the direction of her voice. Just as he did, an arrow pieced his shoulder blade and continued through his chest to exit just below his collarbone.

He gasped at the sharp, tearing pain and staggered forward a step. The vampire he'd been fighting backhanded him across the face, sending him to land on his back in the shallow water at his feet.

He blinked and tried to clear his vision, tried to see through the drunkenness that seemed to be taking over him. Silver. It had to be laced with silver.

His limbs were becoming too heavy to move. The water soaked his clothes and seeped into his ears, making his body feel cold. Glancing up, he stared into Sebastian's contorted face.

"Serves you right, you bastard," Sebastian hissed and held up the crossbow. "Isn't this what you did to me?"

Sebastian stepped over him, straddling his hips to glare down at him in hatred. The rite hadn't been completed; his face still missed part of its skin, and one eye still appeared charred.

"You turned on me, Julian," he snarled.

"I was never with you. I never wanted to be a part of your sick plot and you know it."

Sebastian bared his teeth. "I think it's time I put you out of your misery."

Julian watched in stunned silence as a silver arrow partially exited Sebastian's chest, sticking out just inches where it remained lodged in his chest. Sebastian raised his hand to grasp the arrow, his breathing harsh and erratic as he struggled to remove it, but Julian knew it wouldn't do any good. The silver-laden arrow had already pierced his heart.

Sebastian fell to the side on his back, his dull, lifeless eyes staring straight up at the ceiling. His hands trembled as they continued to tug at the arrow in vain. Marcus moved to stand over him, a crossbow in his hands.

"I figured I owed you," Marcus said, making Julian snort. "Most everyone is taken care of."

"Addison?" Julian asked, almost afraid of the answer he would receive. He'd been terrified they hadn't gotten there in time.

"She's fine." Marcus swallowed, glancing away quickly.

"What?" Julian asked as he tried to stand, but he couldn't seem to move.

Marcus grasped his hand and helped him to his feet. Julian leaned heavily against his son as he looked for Addison. He finally found her sitting on the table, and his heart dropped into his stomach. Her tear-filled eyes met his. Across her lap lay Andre, white as a sheet and barely breathing.

"What do I do?" she whispered, her small body shaking with silent sobs. "I took too much."

Addison could hardly breathe, she hurt so badly. Not physically, but emotionally. She'd been too weak and took too much of Andre's blood. He barely held on to life, and it was all her fault.

Her stare moved to her father's body as it trembled on the floor. She snarled, her demeanor going from fear to anger and hatred in a split second. It wasn't her fault. It was his. Every bit of it. Moving Andre's body, she stood and walked on shaking legs to her father.

"You," she snarled, kicking her foot against his side. He groaned but didn't move. "You son of a bitch! Because of you, I killed him!"

"Addison," she heard Julian caution from behind her, but she ignored him, instead searching for anything she could use as a weapon.

She saw an ax hanging on the wall a few feet away. It hung in the glass case, along with a fire extinguisher. With the palm of her hand, she smashed through the glass, ignoring the tiny cuts that healed instantly. Her vampire powers were at their full strength now, and she could feel all that power rolling through her, mixing with all her hatred, anger, and despair. She focused all of it on the one man who'd caused it all.

After grabbing the ax, she stomped back to her father, splashing water as she went. Standing over him, she stared down at the man who'd sired her—the man who'd made her life a living hell.

"Addison," he choked, and she raised her chin, holding her lips tightly closed. "My child."

"I am *not* your child!" she snapped, raising the ax. "I hope you rot in hell," she yelled, then dropped the ax onto his throat.

His head separated from his body, and blood spurted onto the floor with the last beats of his heart. It mixed with the water, turning it red. She backed away, her anger fading and leaving in its place utter despair. As she did, her sobs echoed through the room. She broke down, releasing all her sorrow.

Julian staggered over and caught her to him, holding her close. Her despair choked her, and she cried out in ragged sobs against Julian's chest. "Andre. I'm so sorry... I didn't mean to."

"I know. It's going to be okay, angel. I promise. I love you," he added on a whisper.

* * *

Addison smiled down at Andre as he moved to a sitting position in the large bed. It was so good to finally see him up and about, his color almost back to normal. Once settled, she placed a tray of food across his lap.

"I could get used to this," he said.

"I'm sure you could," Addison replied with a cheeky grin. "But you probably shouldn't. It's only until you're better."

"Yes, but..." Andre began with a deep sigh Addison knew was fake. "I'm still so weak."

"You're still so full of shit is more like it," Julian replied from the doorway, making Addison chuckle.

"So who do I have to thank for my recovery?" Andre asked, as he used the knife and fork to cut his steak—his favorite food.

"Marcus and Rebecca," Addison replied.

Julian sat down on the bed next to him, making the mattress sink slightly. Andre caught the tray just before it began to slip off his lap.

"You weren't quite as bad off as Addison thought you were, and they were able to use magic to help you heal."

Andre shot Julian a sideways glance. "You seem to be over your aversion to magic."

Julian shrugged, not really answering the question. "You seem to be over your anger with me."

Andre frowned. "Not completely. Not yet."

"Fair enough."

"I forgave him, Andre," Addison said softly as she placed her hand on Andre's leg. She felt the muscles jerk beneath her touch even through the blankets.

"Have the two of you talked yet?" Andre asked as he placed a bite of steak on his tongue.

"Yes. Among other things," Julian murmured.

Andre shot him a glare before turning back to his food. "Don't need to rub it in my face, thank you."

Addison chuckled, then met Andre's gaze through her lashes. "We just talked, Andre. Don't listen to him. Neither one of us have left your bedside since you've been here. I swear. I don't know what I'm going to do with the two of you over the next few centuries."

He stopped chewing and looked at her with a questioning gaze full of hope. "The two of us?"

"Yes. It appears Julian has come around and wishes us to be a threesome."

"I see." He turned to Julian. "Is this true?"

Julian nodded. "With certain conditions."

"No conditions!" Andre snapped.

"You're not exactly in a position to argue about this, Andre."

Andre's fork dropped onto the plate with a loud clatter. "The hell I'm not!"

"For crying out loud, Julian, stop goading him!"

Julian looked at her, his face the perfect picture of innocence. "But it's fun."

Addison laughed. She couldn't help it.

"It's good to see you smile," Andre said softly.

She sobered as the last couple of anxious days ran through her mind. "It's good to know I didn't kill you."

Andre snorted. "You should know I wouldn't have let that happen."

"Okay, now you're just being idiotic," Julian replied with amusement.

Andre ignored him. "So what happened while I was out of it?"

"Addison killed Sebastian, Marcus killed Vlad and Sorel, I pretty much killed everyone else," Julian said.

Andre's lips tilted into a half grin. "I can see that. Is this over?"

"As far as we can tell," Addison replied.

"So what's next?" Andre asked.

Addison smiled coyly. "Well, that depends on what you feel like."

Andre's lips spread into a full smile that made her heart flutter. "At the moment, I feel pretty damn good. But just to be on the safe side, I should probably just lay here and let the two of you have your way with me."

Julian grinned. "Maybe you should just lay there and watch while I have my way with Addison."

"I don't think so," Andre replied, then winked at Addison.

"When are the two of you ever going to get over your jealousy?" Addison asked.

"Never," they replied in unison, making Addison smile and shake her head.

No doubt about it. Life with these two would never be dull.

ᘏTHE ENDᘐ

Trista Ann Michaels

Trista lives in the land of dreams, where alpha men are tender and heroines are strong and sassy. When not there, she visits the mountains of Tennessee. Not a bad place to spend a little spare time when she needs a break from all those voices in her head. Unfortunately they never fail to find her.

Breinigsville, PA USA
09 March 2010
233871BV00002B/19/P